SAVING
SOULS

A SIDNEY ST. JOHN MYSTERY

BY CARY G. OSBORNE

GORDIAN
KNOT
BOOKS

ACKNOWLEDGEMENTS

Thanks go to my darling husband for his help in getting this manuscript ready, and to Paul Marek for his expertise with English grammar and punctuation. Thanks also to Patricia Macomber for her work in making this readable.

For information on Cary Osborne, find her on Facebook. If you would like to be added to her email list, contact her at iroshiok@gmail.com.

As she began closing things down, she realized that the preacher was silent. Was he done for the day? Most likely, as the temperature was already dropping further. Was he coming back tomorrow? Not that it mattered.

She gathered her things together, turned out the lights, and set the alarm, then gathered her coat more tightly around her as she stepped out the side door to the parking lot. First thing she noticed was that the pickup truck still sat on the other corner.

Guess he's just folded his tent, she thought. Must be inside the truck, trying to get warm.

There was no sign of exhaust nor engine noise. The depth of the cold made sound seem sharper, so if the vehicle was running, she would hear it.

She shrugged and pressed the remote unlock button on the CR-V. Opening the back door, she put her bags on the seat. As she started to close the door, she heard a sound, a moan. She turned toward the street and made out a black mound lying on the ground near the rear wheel of the pickup. Immediately suspicious, she reached into her purse on the seat and grabbed her cell phone. She closed the car door and walked across the street to investigate.

The glow from the street light wasn't bright enough to see the figure clearly, but in the glow from the flashlight on her phone, she could see that it was the preacher lying there. She dialed 9-1-1, then knelt down to see if there was a pulse. His skin was cool, not surprising given the cold temperature of the air. He'd been dead only a short while, she guessed.

It wasn't long before Sheriff Otis pulled up in his black SUV. He got out and walked over to her.

"Not again, Sydney."

CHAPTER 1

The damned groundhog saw his shadow.

Six more weeks of winter.

Not surprising really, since the polar vortex moved through the Midwest, all the way down to Oklahoma. Sounded more like something from a movie. One of those apocalyptic ones, showing buildings frozen solid and people struggling to survive.

The arguments over global warming, climate change, and weather vs. climate blared from newscasts on radio and TV. All Sydney St. John knew was that it was colder than hell, and next summer would be hotter than hell, and California was looking better all the time.

Her lover, Ben Bartlett, never mentioned the weather in L.A., where he lived. Their long-distance romance depended, these days, on his ignoring the freezing conditions in which she was living and not rubbing it in that he was getting sunshine and wearing short-sleeved shirts. In summer, both were hot, but humidity was higher in Oklahoma.

With a sigh, Sydney turned back to the computer, with the Blair collection finding aid on the screen. Some people might call it a list or inventory. It listed every folder in the twenty-four boxes and described the contents. She'd just made some changes corresponding with the recent work, but there was still a lot to do. The old collection sat in the archives for years, but the original organization wasn't useful and the finding aid not much more than a list of the boxes and folder titles. Many papers were totally out of place, and one of these days she'd have to do a complete sorting.

The Filmore County Archives held dozens of collections

of papers and memorabilia donated by their creators. Most of them documented the work of ranchers and businessmen, along with family records of those who settled and lived in north central Oklahoma. It was her job to organize these collections for use by researchers, including genealogists, historians, and sometimes just the curious. She'd been doing this work for five years in this archive housed in a re-purposed bank building on a corner in the small town of Gansel.

As she saved the file, a cacophony of noise arose outside. It took a moment for her mind to sort out the details. A man's voice blared through a bullhorn, the words distorted by electronic enhancement. Concentrating, the words became clearer as adjustments were made to the volume and other settings.

"Only Jesus can save you," the voice blared. "Seek Him who is love and understanding. Forsake all others. Give up demon drink, drugs, fornicating, gambling ..."

She could hear the words, although coming through the walls and windows, they were a bit blurred. He must be awfully close. She unlocked the front door of the archive and stepped out onto the sidewalk, wrapping her arms around herself to ward off the cold. At least there was no wind.

Diagonally across Logan Avenue, in the empty lot on the corner, a man stood in the bed of a green pickup truck with the tailgate down. Holding a bullhorn, he shouted out his message to the citizens of Gansel, none of whom made an appearance.

He extolled the virtues of believing and the price of not believing. As she listened to the words of hell and damnation, she wondered if he received a permit to set up there. Either way, she wasn't going to call the sheriff's office to find out. The man was doing no harm, although he chose the wrong town and probably the wrong corner from which to deliver his warnings. As cold as it was, some people might welcome the idea of the fires of hell.

Noting that he was dressed warmly and hoping there was some sort of heater in that pickup, she went back inside. About an hour later, looking out the window next to her desk, she saw Bursom, one of the sheriff's deputies, stop and check the man out. Apparently, everything was in order, and the deputy got back into his SUV and drove away. She thought about taking the man a hot cup of coffee, but decided, if he was smart, he brought his own in a thermos. It would be foolish not to on such a cold day. Besides, she didn't want to get involved with him or his type. Religion was one thing she steered clear of, in all its forms.

Just before noon, Sheriff Otis dropped by. He brought cold in with him as he stepped into her office. He refused a cup of coffee.

"I see you have some entertainment today," he said. He settled into her visitor's chair with some difficulty. He was a very large man and dwarfed most furniture. The heavy coat didn't help him to fit between the chair's arms.

"Yes, he got there early. I keep wondering why he chose Gansel to receive his message."

"No idea. He isn't from around here. He has a Colorado license plate. Might be one of those itinerant preachers, going from town to town. People will usually drop a dollar in the cup and move on."

"Did his application have an address?"

"Somewhere in Colorado, too. Maybe he wants to move here."

"He picked a bad time and place to audition," she said. Shivering, Sydney slipped on her sweater as if to emphasize her words.

"Well, I thought I'd check to see if he was being a nuisance," he said as he stood.

"Nah, he's part of the background noise today. I do wonder how long he intends to stay though."

"His permit was for all day. Don't believe anyone can stay out in this freezing weather that long."

"I'd be surprised if he did."

She let him out the door and locked it. His checking things out was the sort of thing she expected after living in Gansel the past five years. He saved her life at least once. She counted him a good friend, yet had never met his wife or knew much else about his family or background. His children were all grown and moved away; that much she did know. One day, they would have to sit down and have a heart-to-heart conversation.

It was nearly half past twelve, and she was meeting Julia, her best friend in town, for lunch at Molly's. She walked over and found the cafe crowded. Spotting Julia in one of the booths against the left wall, she waved, then threaded her way between tables and chairs, greeting acquaintances along the way.

She kept on her coat at first, still trying to warm up from walking the two blocks between the cafe and the archives. They ordered chili, perfect for such a cold day, and exchanged pleasantries.

"Anything new going on today?" Julia asked. She loved gossip, although she didn't readily pass on everything she heard.

Sydney told her about the preacher and his bullhorn. "He was leaving when I locked the door. Guess he was going to lunch, too."

"Is he saying anything new or different?"

Sydney shook her head and waited as Brenda, the new waitress, set their food in front of them.

"No one's listening. Too cold. I can shut out his voice much of the time. When I'm in the processing room, I don't hear him at all."

The processing room of the archives was in the basement, deep in the ground, except for the back where a garage door opened up to the alley. The alley was below street level, and the garage door once admitted armored cars bringing in money and taking some out, depending on the day. That was when the bank occupied the building, until the 1980 market crash.

She described the man and his truck in response to Julia's questions, then they concentrated on eating and talking about their own lives. Neither of them led exciting lives, at least not for a while.

"When is Ben coming back?" Julia asked.

"Not for a couple of months. He will be busy until the end of April at least, and possibly later than usual since he's taken on some new clients. We're still planning his next visit."

"Better thee than me," Julia said. "Long distance romances are hard."

"What about you and Paul?"

"That's different. We're married." Julia laughed, then said, "Sometimes it feels like it actually helps our marriage to be apart some of the time."

Paul was an over-the-road truck driver who was gone during the week and home on weekends. Unless the weather kept him from getting home, which happened twice this winter so far.

They discussed their relationships as they finished their chili, then both went back to their respective workplaces: Julia to her florist shop across the street and down half a block, and Sydney to the archives where she worked alone most of the time. The preacher drove up to the empty lot as she stepped inside. He took up his preaching again, and she returned to planning the organization of another small collection, consisting of seven boxes of business papers.

Why is he here? Her innate curiosity was aroused, but not enough to occupy her for long.

When five o'clock was announced by the chiming of the old school clock in the hall, she was surprised. Her concentration on the papers and the words they contained was often so complete that she became unaware of her surroundings, including the darkness beyond the window.

As she began closing things down, she realized that the preacher was silent. Was he done for the day? Most likely, as the temperature was already dropping further. Was he coming back tomorrow? Not that it mattered. She was curious enough to think of going across to introduce herself and ask his name. Maybe the next time she saw Otis, she might ask him. That was her stock in trade: curiosity and seeking information.

She gathered her things together, turned out the lights, and turned the night lights on. She set the alarm, then gathered her coat more tightly around her as she stepped out the side door to the parking lot. First thing she noticed was that the pickup truck still sat on the other corner.

Guess he's just folded his tent, she thought. *Must be inside the truck, trying to get warm.*

There was no sign of exhaust nor engine noise. The depth of the cold made sound seem sharper, so if the vehicle was running, she would hear it.

She shrugged and pressed the remote unlock button on the CR-V. Opening the back door, she put her bags on the seat. As she started to close the door, she heard a sound, a moan. She turned toward the street and made out a black mound lying on the ground near the rear wheel of the pickup. Immediately suspicious, she reached into her purse on the seat and grabbed her cell phone. She closed the car door and walked across the street to investigate.

The glow from the street light wasn't bright enough to see the figure clearly, but in the glow from the flashlight on her phone, she could see that it was the preacher lying there. She dialed 9-1-1, then knelt down to see if there was a pulse. Checking the carotid first, she detected nothing. His skin was cool, not surprising given the cold temperature of the air. He'd been dead only a short while, she guessed.

When the emergency operator came on line, she asked for an ambulance and the sheriff. She stamped her feet, trying to keep them from going numb while she waited.

It wasn't long before Sheriff Otis pulled up in his black SUV. He got out and walked over to her.

"Not again, Sydney."

CHAPTER 2

When she told Ben about the death over the phone that night, he wondered aloud how she kept getting into these situations.

"Just lucky, I guess," she said.

He laughed. "I'd rather you were a little less lucky myself."

She agreed. "Not certain how I can keep it from happening."

"You could move out here."

She groaned. "I knew what you would say as soon as I spoke."

"Yeah, well …"

"I'm still thinking about it. Maybe if you moved here instead, these things wouldn't keep happening."

He groaned in turn.

They left the subject of the murders that she'd been associated with last year and talked about more current happenings. Tax season was going hot and heavy, and he was working long hours. His reputation as a tax accountant was growing since some of his clients, well known in the movie business and others who were rich investors in other fields, were spreading the word that he worked miracles. The previous tax season, he saved one of his clients from going to jail because of a political contribution that turned out to be suspicious.

He made a very good living, which made possible the many trips to Oklahoma to see her. For now, however, and for the next several months, his business would keep him in California. They were talking about her taking a week's vacation in March to visit him. Then, there was an archival conference in San Diego coming up in April and she hoped to mix business with pleasure.

They hung up after an hour as usual. They would talk again on Friday, as was their habit, unless one of them wanted to discuss something that couldn't wait. Such as her finding the body of a preacher.

Next morning, Sydney was distracted, half expecting Otis to call and let her know the cause of death of the preacher. She was also curious about the man himself, whether he had any family, where he came from, why he stood out in freezing weather to preach on a street corner with no one listening. Although Otis accepted her curiosity about the earlier two murders she was involved in, this time it was nothing to do with the archives.

The one thing that kept eating at her was the moan she heard when she was at her own car. Was the man dead long enough for his body to have cooled when she checked him? So, who moaned and why hadn't she wondered about that earlier?

It might be assumed the preacher died from exposure given the weather. Past experience made her doubt it.

By mid-afternoon, she could stand it no longer and called the sheriff's office. Otis was in and the deputy on the desk transferred the call to him.

"Sydney, what can I do for you?" Before she could respond, he said, "I bet you want to know who the itinerant preacher was and why he was in Gansel."

"You know me too well, Otis. Did he die of exposure?"

"Now Sydney ..."

"Come on, Otis. You know I'll help any way I can. And I did find the body."

"True. But that doesn't give you *carte blanche* in a murder investigation."

She realized that he was telling her without really telling her.

"How?"

"Just because there was a knife wound—it could have been self-inflicted."

"Right."

"I can give you his name since that will be made public in tomorrow morning's papers. It was Patrick O'Kelley. He was fifty-two and not an ordained minister."

She wrote down the information as he talked.

"Was he affiliated with any particular church or group?"

"Not that we've discovered."

"Anything in his truck that would ..."

"There wasn't much; I can tell you that. It didn't look like he was living in his truck, though."

"Okay. The name 'O'Kelley' sounds familiar."

"I believe it's a good old Scotch/Irish name."

"No not that. Something in Oklahoma history. I'll figure it out," she added after a moment's thought. "Thanks, Otis."

"Let me know what you find, if anything." He knew she would start digging.

"Sure."

"Be careful, Sydney. I don't want you getting involved again."

"I know. Ben's already warned me."

They said goodbye after a few more words of warning from Otis. She leaned back in her chair, tapping the eraser end of the pencil on the desktop. The name O'Kelley definitely was familiar. She signed onto the Internet and began searching.

Her first search term—O'Kelleys in Oklahoma—brought up a name that was vaguely familiar: Edward Capeheart O'Kelley. The man who shot Bob Ford, who was the man who shot Jesse James.

As she read his biography on *Wikipedia*, she kept trying to remember where she might have heard or read the name before. Maybe it was in one of the collections, some mention of the name by one of the people whose papers she organized. Perhaps in some earlier research into state history.

The *Wikipedia* article described how O'Kelley found Bob Ford in Creede, Colorado where Ford owned a saloon housed in a tent after the first building was destroyed. O'Kelley, known to some by the name "Red," walked up behind him and shot him in the head with a shotgun. Thinking he would be hailed as a hero, O'Kelley didn't try to get away and ended up spending nine years in Colorado State Prison, much to his chagrin. After his release, O'Kelley eventually settled in Oklahoma City. In 1904, he got into a fight with a city policeman, Joe Burnett, and after a "prolonged fight," O'Kelley was shot twice and died immediately. He was buried in Oklahoma City.

Sydney wondered if it was because of a reference to the grave in the cemetery in Oklahoma City that made his name sound familiar since the details of the fight and burial were well documented. No explicit memory of finding it came to mind, however. A trip to the cemetery might be interesting.

She pulled up short at that point. There was no indication that the recently murdered man was connected at all to Edward O'Kelley, in spite of his last name. No use in going off half-cocked just yet.

The rest of the week was busy, with several researchers in the reading room each day. Dr. Berger was back, in the early stages of studying Route 66. He hadn't yet told her what his angle was, but he must have a different one since so much literature existed already on the iconic highway.

A few strangers appeared, drawn to the location of the murder. Since the information released to the newspapers by Sheriff Otis's office identified her as the one who found the body and was published in *The Oklahoman*, curious people hoped to get her story of what happened. Between them and local reporters, she repeated the same response a dozen times or more. "Everything I know is in the article." They grumbled and left or hung up. She watched some of them through her office window as they took pictures of the empty lot, where the yellow crime scene tape fluttered in the cold wind.

In addition to helping the researchers in the archives, Sydney was working on an article of her own for one of the scholarly journals dealing with professional archival issues. Given that two collections she dealt with were twice the basis for murder, she thought it would be interesting to study the effects of past lives on present ones. She didn't plan it as a sensational piece, but no matter how she wrote it, it might be seen as such. The problem was figuring out how to keep that from being seen as the *raison d'etre*. She might need help with that part.

By early Friday afternoon, the reading room was empty and she cleared up all of the required paperwork. Once that was done, she worked on Internet research, enjoying the opportunity to relax.

For a change, she closed up exactly at five and headed for Molly's Café, around the corner and down the street, to meet Julia. They didn't usually eat together twice in one week, but Julia's husband, Paul, was on a longer trip than usual, and Julia, for all her independence, was lonely.

In spite of the cold, Sydney decided to walk, feeling the need for some exercise. The wind was calm, but the cold penetrated her wool coat. By the time she reached the cafe, her fingertips and nose were numb. Her ears would have been, too, if it weren't for the stocking cap she pulled down low. She hated gloves and hats, but if the weather held, she would have to get used to them.

It was a bit early for the dinner crowd, and Julia wasn't there yet, so she found an empty booth against the wall on the left, out of habit. She shed the winter paraphernalia and tossed everything on the banquette, where she sat facing the door. She ordered hot chocolate, and as she waited, a few more familiar residents came in. Julia came through the doorway and moved across the room, greeting people on the way. She always looked healthy and happy, and now the cold turned her cheeks pink, adding to the natural glow.

"How goes it?" she asked as she began disrobing.

"Great," Sydney said. "It's Friday and it's cold as hell."

Julia smiled and sat down. She rubbed her hands together.

"So, have you learned anything else about our murdered man?" Julia asked. This was partly the reason for her invitation to have dinner together, of course.

"Nothing so far."

"Come on. You found the body."

"Yeah."

"Nothing in the archives? No family connections?"

Brenda came over at that moment and took their order. Once the waitress left, Sydney told her friend everything she knew so far.

"What do you plan to do now?" Julia asked.

"What makes you think I'm going to do anything?"

"I know you. You can't stand not getting involved. You'll research or something, wanting to help Otis figure it out."

"Don't forget the last two times I've gotten involved, there were connections to collections in the archive. As far as I know, this guy has no connection to any of the papers."

"You are going to look around, aren't you?" It was a statement rather than a question.

"Well, I want to go to the cemetery and check out the grave of this Edward O'Kelley. But I have no idea if the two men are connected."

"O'Kelley isn't that odd a name."

"I know, but ..." She shrugged.

"I'll come with you."

"Won't Paul be home this weekend?" She knew he wasn't arriving that night but expected he would be home by Saturday. Winters often made his job a bit more unpredictable.

"He's in Dakota somewhere. I forget whether it's north or south. He won't be home until next weekend."

"That's two weekends in a row, isn't it?"

Julia nodded.

"It's pretty cold out there," Sydney said, watching as Julia raised one eyebrow. "In the cemetery, I mean."

"Don't try to discourage me."

"Oh, I'm not." Sydney sighed and rested her elbows on the table. "Why don't we meet tomorrow morning. My house. We can take my car down to the cemetery, then maybe have lunch, do some shopping... Sound good?"

"Sounds great." Julia smiled.

Sydney nodded, leaning back just in time to have her dinner set before her.

With dinner finished and their plans made for the next day, they walked together until they reached the flower shop. "See you in the morning," Julia said as they parted. Sydney felt the excitement she always felt when going off on a new research project. There was so much to learn, and nothing could go wrong this time.

CHAPTER 3

It was cloudy, and the wind was up next morning when Julia pulled up in front of the house in her four-door pickup truck and got out. It was nine o'clock, and Sydney was ready with the old CR-V running to warm it up. She stepped out onto the front porch, locking the door behind her, then pushing the storm door to. It still didn't work quite right after nearly being torn off its hinges almost two months ago. Julia handed her a cup of coffee in a Styrofoam cup as she climbed into the old SUV. The heater had done its job, and Sydney patted the dashboard with real affection. The car was getting old and a little cranky, but as long as it ran, she would keep it.

They drove through Gansel and merged onto I-35. Since the cemetery was in northwest Oklahoma City, Sydney chose to go through Edmond to Broadway Extension, then south. Between the printout of directions and Julia's GPS app, they made only one wrong turn. The cemetery gates were open, so she drove through. Sudden memories of another cemetery in frigid weather came to her, and she shivered in spite of the warmth coming from the heater.

"So, what's his name, and how do we find his grave?" Julia asked.

"Edward Capeheart O'Kelley." She stopped and pulled a sheet of paper from her book bag. "There's no monument, just one of those low-to-the-ground plaques. There's an office, but it's closed on Saturdays."

She moved the car forward again. The Internet gave her a vague idea of where the grave was. Like many cemeteries, the older graves clustered toward the rear of the property, the newer ones closer to the entrance. She drove deeper into the grounds.

"What's the plan?" Julia asked.

"His grave is in the pauper's section, so there won't be many headstones. Just the same low markers. I tried to find a map or something online but could only get a general idea where the pauper's section was."

After twenty minutes of driving, climbing out to check dates, and walking up and down between rows, Julia finally shouted for Sydney. Standing in front of the grave, she read the name aloud.

"That's it," Sydney said.

The story on the Internet was that a large stone monument was placed somewhere in Missouri to memorialize O'Kelley's life and death. They both wondered why it wasn't put here, where he was buried.

"Now what?"

"I'll take a couple of pictures just for the record and make a note of where it sits in the cemetery. I don't think I'll need to find it again but you never know."

Julia stepped back so Sydney could take the pictures. After a couple of snaps, Julia said, "There's someone watching us."

"What?"

"Over there on the road. The white car."

Sydney looked over her shoulder. A white car with the driver's side window down sat on the paved roadway about fifty feet away. With the heavy clouds, it was too dark to see inside the car, and she made out little more than the silhouette of a man. He seemed to be watching them, but she couldn't tell for sure. A moment later, the window started up and he drove away.

Just another curious cemetery visitor, she hoped. Even so, she pulled out a notepad and pen and wrote down part of the license number, the make of the car, and color.

Julia shrugged, and then they spent a few minutes walking up and down the row of graves, getting familiar with it. A lot of history was written on the tombstones nearby, always a fascination for Sydney. It wasn't long, though, before they both decided it was too damned cold and made their way back to Sydney's car.

It took several minutes to warm up, as they drove to the restaurant where they planned to have brunch. Their conversation was lively, but in the back of her mind, Sydney wrestled with whether to pursue information on O'Kelley.

He wasn't important in the archives since there were no papers and none were likely to come to them. A quick search of the existing inventories showed some mention of him in two other collections.

After the last two adventures—one the spring of last year and the other just two months ago—she really didn't want to face any more. Unfortunately, her curiosity was already aroused, and she told Otis she would do any research he needed. She'd just sit back and wait until he asked.

They visited a bookstore and a department store after lunch, and it was late afternoon when Sydney pulled into her driveway. They hugged and promised to have lunch one day the following week. Julia wasn't sure exactly when Paul might get back, so her plans were a little up in the air. Also, she was doing flowers for a big wedding next weekend, so big it might pay the bills for her shop for two months. Sydney knew the family slightly, had even received an invitation, but weddings weren't her favorite things. Especially going to one alone.

She waved as Julia drove away, her thoughts having turned to Ben and their long-distance romance. She looked forward to his call in the evening, postponed from Friday to today.

After putting away coat, accessories, and purchases, she went to the laptop sitting on her desk in the second small bedroom. She booted it up, then went to the floor-to-ceiling bookcases along one wall and looked over the Oklahoma history titles.

It was in chapters on Oklahoma City history where she found mentions of Edward O'Kelley, or "Red" as he was called. Every article told his history with slight variations. Even so, information about him was fairly skimpy. As she ran her fingers along other titles, one caught her attention. The subject was hidden treasures in Oklahoma. Outlaws were fond of Oklahoma Territory in the late 1800s when there was little law to be found. The book had set unread on her shelf for a year or more; now might be a good time to at least skim its contents.

Searching on the computer for further sources, a single published biography came up. It was a small paperback, self-published, and priced at $40 or more. At that moment, there were no copies available on the Internet, which didn't matter since she didn't have a desire to spend that much on the slim volume for which she might not have any further use.

She put it on her to-do list to check further next week. Eventually, she was sure to find a copy available, but there was no guarantee she would be able to afford it.

Stymied on that front, she turned to the hidden treasures book. It was a subject she knew little about, never having come across anything in the papers or any mention in articles she researched. She was surprised and delighted to find reference to a family named O'Kelley and a treasure hidden in their hog pen. The account was short, but very interesting in spite of that.

On an afternoon in 1917, Mrs. O'Kelley was home alone. Two men knocked on the door, asking about some hogs she and her husband had for sale. She told them they were in the pen and to go ahead and look them over.

She forgot about them until she heard them riding away near dark. Thinking it was strange they had been there so long, she kept about her business until Mr. O'Kelley got back home. She told him about the visitors, and although it was very late by then, he took a lantern to inspect the pen. There he found a deep, wide hole where a large rock had been buried. Next to the hole was a lard bucket that obviously was buried in that same hole.

Upon inspecting the bucket, Mr. O'Kelley determined that impressions of twenty-dollar coins were pressed into the bottom, and a few more impressions up the sides. Later, he estimated there would have been approximately $30,000 in gold. He reported the incident to the sheriff.

Mrs. O'Kelley gave a description of the men to the sheriff who found that they recently had been released from prison in McAlester. Later, one of the men's uncle deposited $5,000 in gold in his bank.

Sydney closed the book and sat thinking. Ed O'Kelley died in 1904. Some stories said that he was friends with or married to a cousin of Jesse James. That was one reason given for his shooting Bob Howard: as payback for killing Jesse. If—and it was a big if—Ed rode with Jesse at one time, he might have gotten $30,000 and needed a place to hide it.

Would he have gone to his relatives in Oklahoma and, with or without permission, buried his ill-gotten gains in the hog pen? Would his relatives have known nothing about it? When did they buy the farm? The presence of the large rock on top of the buried treasure must have been pretty obvious. How much would that treasure be worth today? And why didn't Ed go back for it when he got out of prison and moved to Oklahoma City, leaving it to be dug up many years later?

The phone rang, bringing her mind back to the present. It was Ben calling at their usual hour. Eight o-clock already? How had time slipped away like that?

They talked at first about their weeks, although they had spoken a couple of evenings before. When she got to Saturday, Sydney told him about her and Julia's adventure at the cemetery.

"Not really an adventure," she said, amending her first mention, not wanting to tell him about the person in the white car. "We found the headstone and that was about it. Nothing new."

She went on to tell him what she'd learned about Ed O'Kelley from the research, then about the treasure.

"That's pretty exciting," she said.

"You're wondering what happened to the gold."

"Of course. What if someone thinks it's still out there somewhere, still intact? Ed O'Kelley certainly didn't live high when he was in Oklahoma."

"Why wouldn't he if he knew where all of that gold was?"

It was a question nagging at Sydney, too, without a good answer. It was logical to believe that he didn't know where it was, given his lifestyle. Her gut told her that the itinerant preacher was connected to the past in some way through Ed. When she said this to Ben, he wasn't so sure.

"Seems like a stretch to me."

"Yeah, but the name. It may be common in Irish surnames, but it isn't in this area."

"You're getting involved again." Ben's voice said he wasn't

happy about that.

"No, just trying to find information for Otis."

"That's what you always say."

"I know, but this time, I have no connection to the victim at all. It'll be all right."

CHAPTER 4

"Dr. Berger, I wasn't expecting you today."

Sydney stepped aside to let the old scholar pass, then closed and locked the front door to the archives. The cold weather hadn't abated, and she shivered as frigid air entered with him.

"It's too cold to do much else," he said. "Although I think I would have been better off staying at home where it's warm."

"I understand that."

He set his satchel down on the floor and hung his long wool coat on the coat rack next to the bank of cubby holes for personal items. Once he set out everything he needed from the bag, he placed it in one of the cubbies.

"Your box is still on the table," she said. "You'll have the reading room to yourself, unless someone else decides to brave the cold."

He nodded and went inside. Settling himself at the table, he pulled the box close and selected a folder. He had looked through it the previous week and left it there for his return. Sydney went back to her office. She liked him and enjoyed reading his work; it was the good doctor who found something in one of the collections a few months ago that started her on a dangerous course. Hopefully, there were no more such secrets to be found.

On the list for the day were several choices: work on the current collection, finish the changes to the Blair finding aid, or work on the box list of the new collection that arrived last week. There was nothing on the list pertaining to Dr. Arnold, who was off on another trip with his less than adorable wife but she could do more research on the computer. Of course, that meant the O'Kelleys.

She studied the list. The box list for the new collection she would give to Charlene Hooks, her part-time assistant. To work on the newer collection, she needed more folders, which were on order but not yet delivered. The Blair finding aid was, perhaps, of more importance. The adventures earlier in the year, as chronicled in the newspapers, created interest in the archive, bringing a few more serious researchers and just curious folk who came and went the same day, never to be seen again.

One thing to look forward to was the archivists' conference in April. She wasn't presenting anything, so her time would be her own, with a few extra days to spend with Ben. The thought of warm sun and ocean breezes brought a sigh. Thinking of several days in a hotel with Ben brought a blush of excitement. They had known each other nearly a year, and he was already a big part of her life, even though hundreds of miles separated them. No matter what anyone said, she rather liked it that way.

Settling in at the computer, she began searching for anything on the itinerant preacher. Patrick O'Kelley couldn't be a very common name, at least not in Oklahoma. Since he was probably from Colorado, though, the search might be more difficult.

She tried to push aside thinking that he might be related to Ed O'Kelley just because of his last name. None of the information she'd gathered mentioned anything about the outlaw fathering any children. One account suggested he might have married a cousin of Jesse James. The stories differed in details.

There could be other ancestors, of course, perhaps an aunt and uncle who lived in Oklahoma. Was that couple with the hogs related to Ed?

This question would require more genealogical research than usual. It would be made difficult by his parentage being somewhat suspect. The next question was, how close was he to Jesse James? If they weren't related by marriage, was Ed ever actually a member of that or any other of the gangs pillaging the Midwest in the late 1800s, the best known being the Youngers, Daltons, and Jameses? Other lesser-known bands roamed about, too. It was clear from many sources that he wanted to be an outlaw and managed to get in trouble on his own, but there was little about the famous gangs. He also saw himself as a lawman and tried to get a job as a deputy in Oklahoma City. The disparate ambitions handicapped him greatly.

Suddenly, the amount of research seemed overwhelming. Sydney decided to work on the Blair finding aid for a while and let the other drop. It wouldn't seem so bad tomorrow.

"This is Matt Luper with *The Oklahoman*."

"Yes." She remembered him from the time that her intern was killed in the archives.

"I was wondering if I could talk with you about the preacher found dead there in Gansel."

"I don't know anything beyond what the police probably told you."

"But you found the body."

"Yes."

"Did you hear him preaching that day? He was right across the street from the archives, I understand."

"Yes, he was there. No, I didn't hear much of what he was saying."

"But …"

"I move around the building, upstairs, downstairs, through the stacks and the processing room. That took me away from the front of the building. Plus, this is an old bank building. The walls are thick and the windows are new double-panes to keep moisture, heat, and cold from affecting the papers."

"How long was he out there?"

Sydney sighed and considered telling the reporter nothing more, but if an article was published quoting her, maybe someone who knew either the preacher or any O'Kelleys in the area would get in touch. It was a long shot, of course.

"I first noticed him about nine o'clock. He may have started earlier. He left around noon and was back at one."

"Were you aware of when he stopped preaching?"

"Not until I left the building a bit after five."

The silence of late afternoon came back to her. The cold, the silence that lay over the world like a muffler. Although it had been quitting time, town traffic was absent; the sounds of other traffic—out on the interstate and county roads—didn't reach into town. Even the wind was quiet.

"I was putting my bags in my car when I glanced over to the empty lot where he'd been preaching. First, I noticed his pickup was still there. That seemed curious. I scanned the area and saw what looked like a bundle on the ground. It was getting dark and I couldn't see exactly what it was, but I was suspicious and walked across."

"What did he look like? I mean, how was he lying on the ground?"

"He was curled up, as if he was trying to keep warm. I could barely see one side of his face. His eyes were open, at least I assumed both were since the one I could see was open."

"You dialed 9-1-1?"

"Yes. I knelt down to try to find a pulse at the same time. His skin was cold. I don't think he was dead very long."

"Was there any wound visible or trauma?"

"No."

"There must have been blood."

"I couldn't see it. It was getting dark, lots of shadows. And I didn't move the body."

"But when the sheriff—Otis—arrived ..."

"I left shortly after the sheriff got there. I didn't see any more."

"Have you talked with him since? Otis, I mean."

"Yes, but he couldn't tell me anything."

"Did the victim's name mean anything to you?"

"No. I don't even know if he's from this area."

"He isn't, at least as far as I've been able to determine. But it has been difficult trying to find out anything about him."

She knew that much but didn't want to tell that to the reporter. It meant admitting to being interested and checking out the history. Luper went on to tell her what little he found, which was little more than she knew. However, he didn't mention the O'Kelley farm and gold coins.

"I don't suppose there is anything in the archives that would be of interest." He was fishing, probably because of the prior two murders involving her and the papers.

"Not really," she said. "I think I've seen the name O'Kelley a few times. I haven't really looked to confirm that." That wasn't true, either, and she hoped he would hang up soon, so she could stop telling half-truths.

"May I call again to see if anything more comes up?" Luper asked.

"I doubt there will be anything more."

Luper laughed. "You do have a reputation for getting involved in murder investigations."

She emphasized that this murder had nothing to do with her or anything in the archives, then said goodbye.

For several minutes, Sydney sat thinking about the conversation and the man who died. His death did not affect her or the archives, yet she couldn't help wanting to find out who he was. Where did he come from? Why was he on a street corner in freezing temperatures, preaching to no one?

She called Charlene Hooks, her part-time assistant, and asked her to come in for a few days to work up the box list on the new collection. It consisted of only seven boxes, mostly cardboard bank boxes, and wouldn't require much time to make up the list and re-folder and re-box it all. Charlene was available the next week and promised to be in bright and early on Monday.

That settled, she pulled up an existing finding aid on the computer and began searching for the O'Kelley name.

CHAPTER 5

The small wood frame house was chilly in spite of the best efforts of the fire in the wood burning stove. The living room was livable, but the two bedrooms didn't benefit as much from the heat, as drafts kept the air moving in through the cracks.

The building, once painted white on the outside, leaned a bit to the right when seen from the road and the screen door was half off the hinges. Newspapers taped over the windows provided some privacy and held back some of the cold wind. It usually housed up to eight illegal immigrants looking for work in the area or working at temporary jobs. They did a lot of landscaping and construction work in town but the prolonged cold this winter sent them back to Mexico or wherever they came from to the south, where it was warmer. They'd be back in spring, unless the atmosphere for immigrants got worse in the States.

Two men sat at a rickety dining table that never saw a good day, eating takeout breakfast sandwiches from the convenience store down the road. They were not illegal immigrants or day workers. They did not work landscaping or construction jobs.

"I sure expected to find more info in his stuff," Saw said. He was tall, evident even when he was sitting, and looked like he'd once been well-muscled. Although the muscle had gone to fat some time ago, he still looked impressively strong. His dark wool jacket was open as they sat near the fire. His full name was Sawyer Buckner.

"Maybe he didn't have anything," Aldo said. He was slightly smaller, also muscular, although a bit of a pot belly showed where his jacket, too, was open. His full name was Aldo Ruvolo.

"Maybe he was full of shit, just thought he was going to find that money."

"I don't know. He seemed pretty certain. The boss believed him."

The big man finished his sandwich and wadded up the paper. He opened the door of the stove and threw it in where it burst into flames immediately. The coals glowed bright red and yellow flames danced through the opening.

"There were s'posed to be papers of some kind. You reckon he lied about 'em?" Aldo asked.

"Maybe. We checked everything—the truck, his bags, that old house he was stayin' in."

He opened up the newspaper he picked up along with the food and began reading. After a few moments he said, "Look here."

He folded the paper so that the second page was on top and turned it on the table so that his companion could read the article. It was about the preacher's murder.

"What's got you so excited?" Aldo said after glancing at the story.

"The archives. The woman who runs it. They got people's papers."

"You're thinking she might have what we're looking for?"

"Could be. Could very well be."

Sydney cursed as she spilled coffee on the steps. Served her right for trying to carry everything inside at one time. Truth to tell, she did as much nearly every morning, usually with better results.

Trying again, she managed to get the door unlocked and step inside. She left the door open as she first went into the little break room and set the paper coffee cup on the counter. Leaving everything else on the chair, she went back outside and picked up the book bag she'd set on the steps, went back inside, and closed the door behind her. She went around the corner and unlocked her office. She set the book bag and purse on the desk, took off her heavy wool coat and hung it up on the coat tree, then retrieved the morning newspaper and cup of coffee, once she wiped it off. She sighed with relief. Just getting into the office was sometimes the hardest part of the day.

She turned on the computer, and while she waited for it to boot up, she spread the newspaper on top of her desk and sipped the coffee. Although she enjoyed her own brew most of the time and everything she needed was in the break room, she sometimes picked up a cappuccino at the convenience store when she picked up the *The Oklahoman* or got gas. For machine made-coffee, it was pretty good and a nice break from her own.

The Oklahoman, however, wasn't her idea of a good newspaper. In fact, more than once, it was called the worst newspaper in the country in various journalism publications. It was one of the few newspapers still being published in the area, and it was the best source of state happenings, many of which couldn't really be called news, but what the hell.

She turned to page two and immediately noticed the headline below the fold: "Archivist only witness to brutal murder."

"Oh, great!"

The article itself did not say that she'd witnessed the murder, only that she was the one who discovered the body. Probably everyone would understand the difference. Would whoever wielded that knife understand the difference?

Damn you, Matt Luper, she thought. What she really wanted to do was call him and shout it out to him but that wouldn't change the possible damage he may have caused. He'd probably say the editor wrote the headline anyway. No use in asking for a retraction or correction. Those editors weren't known for getting things right, even on the second try.

Not to mention what Dr. Arnold was going to think if he saw the headline. She'd been in enough newspaper articles over the past year and none of it good. She could only fume about it for a while and hope that the killer didn't see it. Or believe that she actually saw him or her commit the murder.

She was still fuming when the mail arrived. Mail was something she always looked forward to. As a child, she sent off cereal box tops and Ovaltine liners with a quarter or fifty cents to get plastic submarines that would rise and fall in a sink full of water when filled with baking soda, and other gimmicks promoting shows. She could identify with the Li'l Orphan Annie magic decoder Ralphie so looked forward to in the movie *A Christmas Story*.

There were the bits of advertising and professional catalogs, a white business-sized envelope, probably a request from a researcher for information, and a nine-by-twelve-inch brown envelope addressed simply to "Archives, Gansel, OK." No return address. Nor could she read the date in the red ink of the cancellation stamp, although the name of the town, Corn, was legible. She sat poised with the letter opener in hand, curious about what was inside, and with a slight apprehension. Why did the envelope give her such pause?

Finally, she slit it open. Before pulling out the contents, she got the white cotton gloves used to handle photos without leaving finger prints.

Pulling out the contents, she carefully set the papers on the center of the desk and laid the envelope aside. On top was a note in handwriting so bad it was barely decipherable. Years of practice reading bad handwriting helped, but it still took several minutes.

"These papers are of great value. Other people are after them. Would you take care of them for me until I can reclaim them? Thank you. Patrick O'Kelley."

Sydney wasn't positive about each of the words, but the idea was clear. In her work, she was very accustomed to having to interpret what was meant to be written, without putting words into anyone's mouth.

These would have to be turned over to Sheriff Otis. Could he get fingerprints off of them? She couldn't remember if that was possible with paper. She kept the gloves on. One by one, she glanced at each page, then turned it over into a pile. There were copies of newspaper articles, original articles cut from newspapers, and various other pieces, including hand-drawn maps and handwritten bits on various types of cheap paper.

Some were clearly old and a few bore dates. Two of the articles were published in 1917. One was an account of the mysterious visit to the O'Kelley farm that Sydney read in the treasure book. Two documents were copies of stories about Ed

O'Kelley.

In spite of her better sense telling her to just turn the whole thing over to Otis right now, she took the time to copy it all for her own use. The sheriff would probably be furious that she was tampering with evidence in a murder case, but in the end, she knew he would ask for her assistance. At least, she thought he would. His department was a small one, and often he and his deputies were overwhelmed with the day-to-day problems they handled. She was an experienced researcher, and her skills at ferreting out information served them well more than once. Twice to be exact. Both times she was directly involved in the investigations, to the detriment of her own safety, in fact.

There was also the need to preserve the historical facts contained in the narratives. Protecting them in the Archives was her duty, one she took very seriously.

It took half an hour to copy everything. Some of the pieces were so faint that it took several tries to get a legible copy. Then she called the sheriff's office. Otis wasn't in. She told Sharon, the dispatcher and clerk, that she needed to see him. It was mid-afternoon when he called.

"What's up, Sydney?"

"Hi, Otis. Thanks for calling. I got some papers in the mail today from the preacher."

"How did you manage that?"

"I didn't. It just arrived in the mail. Addressed to the archives, with no return address."

"I'll be right over."

He hung up before she could give him any details. True to his word, his black SUV pulled up at the curb a few minutes later. As soon as she saw his vehicle through the window, she jumped up from her desk and went to the door, unlocked it, then stepped aside to allow his large bulk to pass through the hall.

"It's in my office," she said.

He stood aside in turn, letting her go in first. As she went around the desk, he sat in the wooden library chair that was dwarfed by his size. She handed the envelope to him.

"I don't think I have any gloves that will fit you."

He nodded and pulled a pair of latex gloves from a jacket

pocket.

"Have you looked at them?" he asked.

"Yes. Nothing indicated who sent them or what was inside. I used gloves just in case. There's a note on top signed by him, asking me to take care of the documents. He intended to come pick them up at some later date."

Otis nodded as he carefully pulled out the papers. Sydney cleared that side of her desktop to make room to lay them out.

"I can't make head nor tails of this," he said as he tried to read the note.

"His handwriting is a challenge."

She handed him a printed page from the transcription she'd typed into the computer.

"What do you make of it?" Otis said.

"A little difficult to tell. His handwriting is so illegible I can't tell if he actually spelled anything right. If I interpreted correctly, he might have been a high school graduate." She spread her hands to indicate it was anyone's guess. "As for asking me to take care of the documents, he must have known that he might be in danger, or at the very least, that someone was after what he knew."

"I'm guessing you already did some checking on him. Find anything interesting?"

She smiled. "Yeah, I know you told me not to get involved …"

"Uh huh. But you never listen."

"Hey, the other two times, I was already involved."

"And this time, you're not."

"I know. But I get curious. And, yes, I did some research."

She handed him the folder with printouts of information from the Internet. Also included were a copy of the story of the gold coins from the book, a bit about Ed O'Kelley, and some random notes on O'Kelleys in Oklahoma.

"You have been busy. Why concentrate on this Ed O'Kelley?"

"The story of his being killed in the preacher's papers and the preacher's last name. It rang a bell and I made a connection. There must be one, but I haven't found it yet."

"Well, it could be a coincidence. You can keep the copies you made," he said as he got up from the chair.

"How did you…"

He smiled at her. "Did you come to any conclusions as to what they're about?"

"No, I haven't seen anything yet that would explain why he was here or why he was murdered. The timeline is a problem if you factor in the gold and C.T. O'Kelley."

He told her to keep looking and left. She locked the door after him.

The rest of the day, Sydney spent looking through the papers, checking information out on the Web, and making notes on what she found. She found there really was a C.T. O'Kelley living outside of Delhi, Oklahoma in Beckham County. There wasn't information at all on him or the farm; most of what she knew was from the chapter in the book, and nothing showed them to be one and the same. The county seat of Beckham County was Sayre, created in 1907, the same year Oklahoma became a state.

There were so many conflicting facts about Ed O'Kelley that she doubted anyone knew the whole truth of his past. Maybe his biographer, who was also his great-great niece, had an idea.

Did he marry a cousin of the Youngers as some chroniclers claimed? Other sources said he married a cousin of the James brothers. The facts that everyone agreed on were that he killed Bob Ford in Creede, Colorado, spent time in prison for that crime, eventually moved to Oklahoma City, where he died at the hands of a police officer.

He hadn't expected to spend time in prison for the murder of Bob Ford, believing people would see him as a hero, avenging Jesse James. Once in Oklahoma City, he was suspected of participating in several robberies, all the while hoping to be hired as a city policeman. His end was predictable, as he was known to run with thieves and train robbers.

There was absolutely no further information on the gold coins, the names of the men who dug up the lard bucket, and whether Ed O'Kelley knew about any of it. C.T.—or Charles, as she discovered—and Ed could be from totally different families, thus making any connection with the gold non-existent.

Sydney was beginning to believe there was no connection between Patrick O'Kelley, itinerant preacher, and Ed O'Kelley, outlaw from the past. It was purely a coincidence that both died in central Oklahoma. It must be a coincidence that C.T. O'Kelley and his wife also lived in Oklahoma, although in the western part of the state. Even if there were a connection, it might never be proved.

She sat back, looking at the computer screen in disgust. She didn't much believe in coincidences. All the potential information at her fingertips and there was so little on this one subject. Tomorrow, she would check the city library for a copy of the biography.

There were other books she could check out that cost less than the biography. They included stories about Ed O'Kelley and other outlaws or interesting characters of both the west in general, and Oklahoma in particular. She read a lot of Oklahoma history as background for the information in the papers in her care. Researchers appreciated the additional facts she accumulated in three-ring binders and, through them, being able to place events within the context of the times.

Sydney did a search in the online finding aids for any mention of Ed O'Kelley, in case someone mentioned him in their papers. All that turned up were a couple of mentions of newspaper articles on his death. The fact that he was often in trouble wasn't documented in any of them, as far as she could tell. So many of the finding aids were incomplete, something she tried to remedy when she could; however, new collections came in often enough to keep her busy. Dr. Arnold, her immediate boss, would say she spent too much time investigating murders in the past year. He might be right.

By the end of the day, she doubted that she would find any real connection between the three O'Kelleys.

The only thing to do was to head west to Sayre, the county seat, and check the land records. If the farm existed in or before 1904, her theory might still have a leg to stand on. Proving that, given the date of the creation of the county, was not going to be easy. Otherwise, she would give up on her theory and concentrate on simple research that might help Otis. As far as she could tell at that moment, all avenues were already exhausted.

When she got home that evening, she began another search on genealogy websites while she ate warmed-up leftovers. The difficulties in finding information made her all the more eager to search.

The end of the week came quickly. Several researchers visited the archives, most serious, but a few more thrill-seekers wanting to see the scene of the crime and the person who found the body. In some circles, she was getting a reputation for being involved in violent deaths. Several reporters called, including Luper. She told him that after his earlier article, she wasn't sure she wanted to speak with him. Truthfully, all she could say was that there was nothing new as far as she knew, and they should call the sheriff's office.

Friday, she joined Julia for dinner at the café. Paul was coming in the next morning, so her weekend would be busy.

"What's going on in the old hardware store?" she asked. Julia usually knew everything going on in Gansel, and the empty store front two doors down from her shop, was being renovated.

"Someone is putting in a coffee shop. You know, the yuppie kind." She paused for a moment with her head cocked to one side. "Is that word still relevant?"

"Who knows?" Sydney was enjoying the beef stew, homemade in all the right ways. Although the cold weather was breaking, the temperatures still hovered around freezing during the day. It was the coldest spell she could remember, but old-timers talked about years gone by when it was worse. The past was either "the good old days," or "worse than anything you see today."

"I'm looking forward to it, in any case," Julia said. "Starbucks will never come in here. Not enough traffic."

For the first time in a while, Sydney was reminded of the three locations of Starbucks in Norman when she lived down there and how much she missed them when she moved.

"By the way," Julia said. "What are you doing about a new house?"

"Not much. It's too cold right now. But I did talk with Desideria about building in that new addition. There isn't much really up-to-date otherwise."

"That would be exciting. Who's the builder?"

Nothing was decided in that area and for the rest of the meal, they discussed what the new house should have, what style, and after past experiences, what sort of security. Sydney's rented house had been broken into and she was threatened on more than one occasion. It was an old house and not secure.

On the way home, she considered how much she liked the old house she was living in. She still owned a much newer house in Norman, now rented out, which would have to be sold to provide the down payment on the new one. She once approached her landlady about buying the rental house, then renovating it, but Mrs. Lester declined the offer. She was a widow, and the rent money was a big part of her income. Sydney was almost relieved; renovations were not her strong suit.

Although Gansel had been Sydney's home for nearly five years now, there was a tenuousness about her position with the archive. Doctor Arnold, when he was around, loved to find fault and warn her that she could be out of a job any time.

Supposedly, Arnold hadn't heard about the latest murder yet. More than likely, he would find out from the mystery person in county administration who regularly fed him information on what went on when he was gone. It was not hard to imagine his firing her the moment he found out she signed the contract for a new house. Lately, his appearances in the archive were becoming even less frequent.

Arriving home, she was met with much noise and accusation. Lewis, her part Maine coon cat, expressed his displeasure at being left waiting for dinner in no uncertain terms. Of course, he always thought he was being left to starve, especially since the vet put him on a diet. The new food wasn't as much to his liking, and he clearly felt deprived.

Dropping everything onto the sofa, she pulled off her coat and added it to the pile, then went into the kitchen to fix his canned food. As she set it on the floor, Lewis bumped her hand in thanks, nearly upsetting the bowl. With his evening meal in place and purring loudly, he gobbled it down.

Sydney put everything else away properly and checked her voice mail. There was a message from Doctor Arnold. She hesitated to listen to it, knowing it was bad news as always.

CHAPTER 6

On Friday night, Ben called at nine. After hellos, he asked about the temperatures.

"The weather report says your temperatures have risen above freezing."

"Almost," she responded. "I think today it hovered between thirty-three and thirty-four. Tonight will be very cold again, though, since there are no clouds at all. How is it there? Or should I ask?"

"No, you probably shouldn't." He chuckled.

A while back, he complained that always having what some people called perfect weather—clear, sunny skies—became boring. Rain was a rare thing and snow would mean the end of the world had come. Even so, he was reluctant to be in Oklahoma in spring, during tornado season, which was the time of year they met the year before, and a tornado hit Gansel. It was a bad year for storms.

When they exhausted the weather subject, she mentioned that Dr. Arnold called.

"Where is he?" Ben knew that her boss was out of town more than he was there.

"He didn't say. He said he hoped that everything was going well and that I wasn't getting into any trouble."

Ben laughed.

"He knows you almost as well as I do."

"Hardly. I got the feeling that something's going on."

"Like what?"

"I'm not sure. He was cheerier than usual and … I don't know … just something in the way he spoke. I'm probably imagining things."

Ben agreed with that last statement. The talk turned to Ben's work and clients. Tax season kept him very busy, what with his high-powered clients, who were growing in number. He loved his work, which Sydney found strange, not being a person who enjoyed working with numbers. He felt the same about history and genealogy, which he thought of as a waste of time. Or did before they met. His grandfather, whose papers were in the archives, held a unique place in Oklahoma history, and in helping her research certain aspects of this background and because of his affection for her, he started to understand the fascination. Which is where the conversation turned.

"How's your hunt going? What's his name, O'Kelley?"

"Yes, Patrick O'Kelley. I'm kind of hitting a brick wall here."

"Nothing interesting about the gravesite?"

"No. There's a large monument dedicated to Ed in Missouri. I've seen pictures of it online, and there's nothing there, either."

"What's next?"

"I'm going to look at the county records in Sayre. See if there's anything on the O'Kelleys in Delhi. Some records are online, but not everything."

"Of course not," he said.

She explained that Beckham county was formed in 1907, the same year Oklahoma became a state. Three years before that, Ed O'Kelley was killed in Oklahoma City. Ten years later the gold was found.

"The time span makes the connections dubious, so this is one mystery I might not be able to solve. Then there's the great-great-niece who wrote a biography of Ed several years ago. It's available online sometimes, but expensive, so I haven't bought a copy yet. I thought I'd see if there's a copy in a library somewhere. It might shed light on the mystery of the gold coins."

She hadn't intended to tell him about Patrick O'Kelley's papers coming to her in the mail. He was never happy about her becoming too involved in murder, this being the third time the fates pulled her into this web. Deciding, however, that it was better he know now rather than later, she told him everything she knew regarding them, which wasn't much. She'd only glanced through them, organized them by type, but the details were yet to be studied. Even so, it was clear they held what could be interesting information.

"Why did he send them to you?"

"I've no idea. Just because it's the archives, I guess. It appears that he mailed them in Gansel the same day he was preaching."

"Do you think that's the reason he was preaching on that particular corner? To be near the archives?"

"No one knows why he was there. Otis hasn't found anything, nor have I. If there's any connection to the earlier O'Kelleys it certainly wasn't in Gansel. What's curious is that he mailed them when he could have just walked across the street and handed them to me."

"Maybe he thought he was being watched. If he was, the watchers might have an idea he mailed that envelope and to whom."

She didn't think so and said as much. Unless they saw the address on the envelope or he told someone what he was going to do, there was no reason anyone would know.

"What about the gold? Any idea where it ended up? Or how much it would be worth today?"

"No idea what happened to it. I did find a website that sells gold coins and looked at the current cost of double eagles. If C.T. estimated the amount correctly, they could be worth over two million today."

"Enough to kill someone over."

"I guess."

She could tell by the tone of his voice that he was becoming anxious about her looking into the O'Kelleys, so she changed the subject. Her plans for the trip to San Diego in late April were coming together. His calendar after tax season was clear, so far. Hotel reservations were made, airline schedules scoped out, and she was very much looking forward to being there.

Ten o'clock came, the time they usually ended their conversations, but he was reluctant to hang up. After a few lame attempts to keep her on the line, it was up to her to end it.

"Ben, look, I know you're worried about my looking into this newest mystery. I'm pretty sure that I won't be any more involved this time than doing some research. I promise to be careful."

"I know," he said hastily. Then, "I know," more softly. "I'm sure Otis is keeping an eye on you."

She laughed. "Probably."

"I just worry," he said. "You're so far away."

"I know."

It was a quarter past ten when they said their "I love yous," then good night. Being the night owl she was, Sydney went into her small bedroom-turned-office and opened up the laptop.

Two hours later, she turned it off and closed it, no nearer to finding out about Patrick O'Kelley than before. Monday, she would try to find out from Otis if Patrick was from Colorado, where the truck was registered, and whatever else his office found out. He did have access to records she didn't, and she hoped enough information could be found there to make a difference. Eventually, he would tell her what he found. Probably.

"Who are you looking for this time, Sydney?"

Maria Cardiel worked in the Oklahoma History Center in Oklahoma City and was always very helpful in finding information on people and places. This time, the search was on for newspapers published in Sayre in Beckham County, where Delhi was located, and Mangum in Greer County, where the uncle lived when he deposited five thousand dollars in the local bank. The Center's ongoing project to scan all of the state's newspapers, old and new, made them more accessible to researchers, but it was an ongoing project.

Maria set her up at one of the computers and handed her the finding aid The database wasn't wholly searchable, but there were ways to find specifics. In this case, the protocol Sydney used in an earlier search was good. She began with the last name, O'Kelley, then progressed from there.

One of the first hits was the article in *The Daily Oklahoman*, the name of the Oklahoma City newspaper at the time, about the shooting death of Ed O'Kelley. That was in 1904, before statehood and before the discovery of gold coins in Delhi.

The story of the digging up of the gold, and that one of the young men who visited the hog farm were just released from prison in McAlester, led her to search for records on prisoner releases of that year. The only new information was in an article that named the uncle who deposited the five thousand dollars: Darnell Belton. It would be a big help if the nephew bore the same last name.

She printed copies of the few pages with information she needed and made notes. There was still no confirmation that the Delhi farm was owned by C.T. before Ed was killed in Oklahoma City. It had to be if Ed was the one who buried the coins. Several items of information were needed: Was there a robbery around the same time? There was almost always a robbery in those days, but thirty thousand dollars was an unusually large amount. Where was it stolen? Was Ed or any of the James Gang involved? Was Ed involved with the James brothers at that time?

A visit to the county clerk's office in Sayre was her next step. It was a bit of a drive, but doable in a single day.

In the end, she left the history center with a good amount of information that lent credence to a few suppositions but answered few questions. One possibility was that Ed was in prison in Canon City with the young man who took the coins. If so, Ed might have told him about the gold, although why would he do that?

There must be a list of prisoners and the dates they were incarcerated? Same for McAlester.

It was after five when she got home. After feeding Lewis, she began a list of the questions, places she needed to visit, individual bits of information she might be able to find online.

On Sunday, Desiderio Diego called. As the realtor helping Sydney with building a house in a new subdivision in Gansel, she kept in touch on a regular basis with information and possible plans. Surprisingly, a few people were moving that far from the cities in which they worked and currently lived, not minding the longer drive when living in the country meant clear skies at night, less traffic, and quieter neighborhoods. Telecommuting helped some of them bridge the distance.

Three houses already neared completion, but with the

cold weather, construction was slow. The ground was frozen enough that digging out the site for her house was too difficult, and pouring the concrete footers wasn't practical. Still, some decisions could be made before spring when the ground would be more amenable. A serious problem might come up if the house couldn't be completed by August, when her lease was up on her present abode.

Desiderio wondered if Sydney would like to look through the model homes in Edmond being put up by the same builder whose work she saw on a real estate search online. She could make decisions about a lot of things while awaiting the start of construction, including choosing the lot on which to build. They agreed to meet at one of the model homes and make a list of what she wanted, including the number of bedrooms and size of the garage.

The money from her old house in Norman paid the rent on the one she occupied in Gansel with a good amount left over. After five years, the amount saved was enough for a down payment. The two of them had gone over the finances, deciding on how much to spend and how big a house, given the current prices.

They also visited model homes and Sydney was delighted with one of the floor plans, which included a built-in office. In addition, it would be great to have a two-car garage, where she could actually put her car inside, especially during bad weather. She rarely used the single car detached garage currently available because the door was so difficult to open and close. It seemed easier to clear off the CR-V each morning.

The weather was very clear as she drove south. It was unusually cold for this late in winter, but climate change was affecting the whole world. At one time, she considered working up an analysis of Oklahoma weather through the words of those whose papers were in the archives. Being farmers and ranchers for the most part, they were always aware of the differences and dangers. One day she would tackle that, she told herself, after completing the other projects and work which kept her too busy.

As she often did, she marveled at the strength and vision

of the people who settled in Oklahoma, although a part of her condemned them at the same time for pushing the Native Americans off their land. The history of the state was such a mixed bag. That's why her work was never boring.

Afterward, Desiderio went back to Gansel and Sydney ate dinner in Edmond. Then, she stopped at Target to pick up a few things on her shopping list.

Rather than thinking about the new house, her thoughts were bound up in the research on the O'Kelleys. When Charlene Hooks, her assistant archivist, came in next, she'd take a trip to Sayre. She needed to confirm a connection between Ed O'Kelley, Patrick O'Kelley, and the gold coins.

CHAPTER 7

Interstate 40 ran straight west between Oklahoma City and Sayre. The countryside was bare this time of year, except for stands of green cedars, creating a stark beauty. In places, one could see for miles in any direction. At twenty-five miles or so from the Texas state line, it was a three-hour drive from Gansel.

Sydney turned off the Interstate and drove into town, following the directions she got from the county clerk. The clerk's office was open five days a week; she'd been afraid they might have limited hours, being such a small area and so far from any big town. When she called to make the appointment, the clerk told her that the office was open during lunch as well, so Sydney could be flexible in her plans.

She arrived at 11:30. The courthouse, where the county clerk's office was located, was a three-story, brick building taking up about half a block. Sydney half expected it to be on a town square, like many small towns in the state, but there was no town square at all. The sheriff's office occupied the first floor. The clerk's office and the county court were on the second floor. Her footsteps echoed along the main hall as she looked for the right door. Two women looked up when she entered.

"Hi, I'm Sydney St. John. I called yesterday."

"Oh, yes."

Gretchen Hanover, County Clerk, came over to the counter, and they shook hands.

"I've pulled some record books for you." She motioned toward a table on the other side of the counter. "And I have a list of card files for you to look through. Which would you like to start on?"

As she talked, she motioned for Sydney to come around, through the swinging gate, to the table. Large land record books lay on the table. The older one covered nearly a century, the second only a few years, beginning in 1917. She elected to start with those.

The office was chilly, although no cooler than her own office in the archives. Either they were saving energy or they wanted to preserve the records. Either way, she kept her jacket on for the first half an hour.

The last records in the older book were dated 1917; she worked her way backward from there. Years of experience looking through such records made scanning down the lists for the O'Kelley name a fast operation. In just over an hour's time, she backtracked to 1909, all in the first book. Sales of land didn't occur often, as ownership changed from father to son. Some families held a parcel of land for three or more generations, especially if they came into the state before the land run.

The second book held records back to 1889. Sydney found what she was looking for in the 1903 records. A farm was sold by a family named Wyrick to C.T. O'Kelley. Bingo!

She wrote down the coordinates, then asked for the plat map. She checked her watch; it was two minutes of two. Sundown came about 5:30, so there was time to try and find the location. She certainly didn't want to be caught out on the prairie after dark, with no idea of the roads and accesses, so she would have to get there quickly if she was to have time to look around.

After Gretchen copied the section of the plat map, Sydney went back to her car to compare the location with the atlas and a map she printed off the Internet. The farm was located several miles to the west. She drove out of town, keeping an eye out for the county roads that should bring her to the farm. She hoped there was still a lane or road off the county road to the farm itself.

The car heater blasted hot air into the CR-V, but it took a while for the car to warm up. She kept her gloves on, although she preferred to drive bare-handed. The landscape stretched out fairly straight and flat, with a few hills. The speed limit was 45, but the road was rough so she kept to 35. After fifteen miles, she turned onto another county road, which should lead to the farm.

It was surprising to see oil well pumps operating along the route. She'd believed that most oil and natural gas was in the northern part of the state.

After a little more than an hour of driving, she turned onto the lane she was certain was the right one. It was a mile long and rough as a cob. The farm appeared to be bare of oil wells, cattle, and everything else except three buildings, with cedar trees in a line on one side to form a wind break. She hoped she wouldn't be caught trespassing. Having found no record of the land being sold by the O'Kelleys, she wasn't certain who owned it.

Up close, she made out a house, a small shed, and a pen of sorts, probably the latter being where the hogs were kept. All were built of wood, with tin roofs, and probably were once painted. The barn leaned to the right and would probably collapse in that direction in a future wind storm. The house looked more as if it collapsed inward, with only the roof to maintain the overall shape. The planks were weathered to grey, resembling iron. The pen was probably where the gold cache was dug up, although now there was probably nothing to find in the pen except maybe the large stone that covered the hiding hole.

The front door was actually closed, much to her surprise. With the collapsed look of the house in general, she expected the door to be hanging on one hinge or something. She pushed it open, cringing at the squeal of rusted hinges. The first room was small, probably a parlor, with two wooden chairs, one leaning on three legs. Curtains were tacked over the windows and now hung in dusty grey shreds. Some of the glass in the windows was still whole, but the wind was free to blow through broken panes. Thank goodness, the wind wasn't blowing at that moment; the temperature outside was cold, but inside the derelict house, it felt even colder.

The room, with its layers of debris, held promise of finding something revealing about its last occupants. She put on her latex gloves, then kicked through newspapers, pieces of wood, a couple of forks, and an old leather wallet that was empty. People evidently had searched through there before, and everything they considered useless was flung to the floor. She did find an old buffalo-head nickel that someone missed.

Sydney stepped gingerly through the room toward the back. A kitchen occupied the left rear of the house, and a single bedroom was to the right. She chose the latter, where an iron bedstead held up a disemboweled mattress, the stuffing nowhere in the room, probably stolen by critters for nesting. A cedar chest sat against one wall, its layers of veneer peeled apart, looking like pages of a book. In the bottom lay a white handkerchief, folded twice, looking pristinely white.

Less debris cluttered the floor than in the parlor and looking through it took little time. Old bed sheets lay in a bunch in one corner, covered with feathers from pillows, along with remnants of clothes, a broken pipe, and unidentifiable bits. Pushing aside a magazine, her heart began pounding in her chest. Sydney cleared a bit more trash, then reached down and picked up a leather journal. Anyone looking for treasure would have discarded this, for which she was thankful.

The leather covers were soiled, and the pages inside were yellowed with age. The writing was in pencil and would take some patience to read, but on first glance, there were no missing pages. The name written on the first page was Anne O'Kelley. She put the journal in her coat pocket, planning to read it later, and searched a little longer in the bedroom, in the end, finding little else of interest.

The kitchen boasted a water pump on a wooden counter and a metal basin probably used to wash up people and dishes. A table sat to one side. It looked sturdy, but she didn't test it. There was no window looking toward the back in the kitchen, and the back door, leading toward the barn and hog pen, hung half open, held by two bent hinges. She tried to push it open further, but it was frozen in place, giving her just enough room to squeeze through if she wanted.

Open drawers held most of the remains, mostly cutlery, and a small pot with a hole in it lay on its side on the floor. Bits and pieces of paper lay about on linoleum that curled upward at the corners. She went into the parlor and picked up the wallet, putting it in the same pocket of her coat with the journal, then made her way out the front door.

The wind blew now, and she buttoned up her coat. Behind the house, two small cedars had taken root in the dirt yard. The hog pen sat to the right, an outhouse further right, and a work shed to the left. Straight out from the back door lay wild land, looking as if it had never been plowed or grazed.

She stopped at the sound of a car moving slowly down the lane, toward the front of the house. It stopped, and two doors slammed shut. Men's voices blew away in the wind. Going to the corner of the house, she tried to peek around, but they weren't in sight from there. Her heart thumped in her chest. As she feared, she was caught trespassing by the owner. She would have to 'fess up. However, past experience told her to wait and see the newcomers before facing them.

The front door of the house opened, the squeal of the hinges loud in the stillness that followed another gust of wind. Footsteps came toward the kitchen and the open back door. Stooping slightly, she made her way along the side of the house toward the front. She hoped to be near the SUV before they saw or heard her, just in case. Pulling the keys from her jeans pocket, she pushed the unlock button. The lights blinked, but at least the CR-V didn't honk when unlocked.

A huge, black SUV, the kind one sees serious law enforcement driving in movies, dwarfed the CR-V. She pulled the car door open as one of the men stepped through the front door.

"Hey!"

She climbed in, put the key in the ignition and started the engine. Then she lowered the window half way.

"We want to talk to you," the man yelled. He walked as he talked, approaching her car.

"I know. I was trespassing. I apologize."

The second man stood just outside the front door, hands on hips, watching. For a moment, she thought she saw a pistol on the belt at his waist.

"What are you doing here?" the first man said.

"I'm interested in history. I thought this was the old O'Kelley place."

"It is." He was beside her door.

"Still?"

"What did you hope to find?"

"Just getting the feel of the place. I recently read a story about this farm and the O'Kelleys and wanted to see for myself."

"What did you find?"

"Nothing."

Without looking away from him, she slid the car into reverse. He was bound to notice, of course, since the sound of the engine changed.

"Are you related to the O'Kelleys?" he asked.

"No."

He looked back at his colleague.

"Sorry I was trespassing," she said. "It's getting late and I need to head home."

His hand moved to pull his coat aside. She waved, backed up quickly, turned, and headed down the lane. In her rearview mirror, she saw them climb into the black behemoth. Checking the gas gauge, she was relieved to see that the tank was half full. Looking in the mirror again, they appeared closer. One saving grace was that dust rose in her wake, so they couldn't read the license number.

Unless they read it and wrote it down when they first arrived. If only it was possible to have gotten their license number. Were they going to chase her? Or just make sure she left? The question she didn't want to think about: did one of them kill Patrick O'Kelley?

CHAPTER 8

She turned onto the road, keeping one eye on the other vehicle in the mirror. It hesitated at the turn and was still sitting there when she made the turn onto the next road. Careful not to drive over the speed limit, she drove through Sayre and out onto the interstate. Heading east, with the sun low in the sky behind, she drove as fast as she dared. When she turned off toward Gansel, she breathed a sigh of relief. No sign of the black SUV and she was now close to home.

She stopped at the new 7-11 and got gas, then drove on home. It was six o'clock and she was tired. Her body still pumped a lot of adrenalin from her fright at the O'Kelley place. All she wanted was to sit down, put her feet up, all the while hoping that whoever the two men were, she'd seen the last of them.

Leftovers sufficed for supper, all the while watching the news on TV. Having eaten his fill, Lewis curled up beside her on the sofa. Even though his eyes were closed and he purred loudly, he seemed unusually alert, possibly because of her own tension that just wouldn't go away.

When the news ended, she turned off the TV and retrieved the journal and a magnifying glass. Turning the three-way lamp up to the highest, she opened the journal. In the more closed atmosphere of her house, the scent of dust and mildew rose to her nose and she sneezed. If it got worse, using a dust mask would be in order.

The pencil used to make notes was not a dark one, and the point was broad so that every letter and word was dim and each stroke overlapped. At nine o'clock, she was halfway through. She stood and stretched, muscles and joints stiff, and her left elbow popped. In the kitchen, she put the dishes in the sink, then moved to the living room to put another log on the fire.

Someone knocked on the door. She tensed. Too many times over the past year, when someone came to her door, she ended up fighting for her life or, at the very least, fighting to keep them out. Today, two men in a black SUV confronted her and threatened her. At least it felt that way. The knock on the door could only mean something bad was about to happen.

She hefted the poker, thinking to use it as a weapon. The newly purchased pistol was in the desk in the office. The knock came again. She tiptoed to the window and peeked between the curtain panels, trying to make out the person on the porch and the vehicle at the curb. The person stood too far to the left. The vehicle was a big SUV, black, glistening in the light of the streetlight at the corner.

The knock came a third time. "Sydney, it's Sheriff Otis. I know you're there."

She nearly fainted with relief. Of course. Otis drove a black SUV. Of course, it was huge.

She unlocked the door and pulled it open. Otis pulled the storm door far enough to accommodate his bulk through the open doorway and stepped over the threshold.

"Evening, Otis."

She put the poker in the rack beside the fireplace, then stepped to the center of the room. He filled her living room more than usual, with his bulk wrapped in a down coat and a furry hat with ear flaps tied at the top, which he pulled off his head.

"Evening, Sydney. Sorry to come by so late."

"It must be important."

"The OSBI thinks so."

"Oh?"

She became familiar with the Oklahoma State Bureau of Investigation during the investigations of the two separate murders last year. The only reason she could think of for their interest in her now was Patrick O'Kelley. She asked Otis if it was about that.

"Pretty much. Two of their agents were out to a farm west of here that once belonged to a family of the same name."

Oh, dear, she thought. *Those two men were OSBI.* She said nothing.

"Seems as though they found you there, trespassing at best."

"They never said who they were."

"I told them that was probably the case, and about your adventures last year. They were not amused."

"I guess they would have chased me down if they were anyone else." She turned to sit back down on the sofa. "Have a seat."

Otis sat in the overstuffed chair that suited his size.

"Did you find anything at the house? They will be even less amused if they found out you took something."

Her eyes cut to the journal sitting on the table beside her, then quickly back to Otis. He glanced in the same direction, and she knew she'd given herself away. She would not have lied to him, in any case.

"It's a journal kept by Anne O'Kelley. I'm trying to read it, but it's tough going."

"I'll have to take it, Sydney. The OSBI has experts for that sort of thing."

"But Otis ..."

"It's private property. I'll convince them not to press charges for stealing or trespassing, which will be easier if I give them the journal."

She sighed and reached for the leather book. She really screwed up this time, and she believed him about the OSBI. Giving up the information that was written down by someone who lived on the farm was crushing to both her curiosity and her desire to help in the investigation.

"May I finish reading the entry I just came to?"

He raised an eyebrow.

"It's about the day the two men came for the gold coins."

She showed him the entry, on three pages, and he put on his reading glasses. Clearly, he couldn't make out much of it, so he handed it back to her.

"Why don't you type it out on your computer and print me a copy."

Without saying the thank you that came to her tongue, she agreed. She brought her laptop into the kitchen while Otis drank a cup of coffee she heated in the microwave for him. The transcription took several minutes, as using the magnifying glass was the only way to be certain of the words. When it was done, she printed the single typed page.

A few minutes later, the sheriff left with the sheet of paper and the journal in his pocket. Sydney went straight back to her office with the laptop and typed out what she remembered of the rest of the journal. The text she managed was more a sense of what was on the pages rather than a word-for-word transcription, but that was what was important anyway.

Obviously, Anne O'Kelley could read and write, but not well; her spelling was minimalistic, and her syntax could only be called creative. The entries were not dated, only designated by the day of the week in chronological order. The newspaper article told her what the date was when the two men went to the farm and dug up the gold coins. Matching the day with the date would confirm the events were the same.

As it turned out, Anne confirmed the events as reported and added slightly more information. The two men who came that night were relatively young. She'd paid little attention as she was busy with her youngest child suffering with a toothache. Some time passed before she remembered they were supposed to be in the hog pen, but Charles came back around that time. After he went to check on them, and found the lard bucket, he was very curious at first, then angry about what appeared to be a cache of gold coins, buried right under their noses, and now gone.

In the earlier entries, Sydney got a sense of the loneliness a woman could feel on a farm in the middle of nowhere with children to keep her tied to the house, while her husband often went into Delhi, the nearest town, to take care of farm business. What else was in the journal, she might never know. It was a good thing the important stuff was near the beginning.

The next afternoon, Otis called the archives to let her know that the OSBI was willing to forget any charges against her. He showed the agent who came for the journal the single page of transcription Sydney did and suggested that if they needed someone to interpret the entire journal, Sydney would most likely be available. She could have kissed him but toned down her enthusiasm to "I'd be delighted." She reminded him that it would also take her less time than another person since she was already familiar with the handwriting and had experience reading difficult handwriting in general.

She was still surprised when an agent and Otis appeared on Thursday with the journal in a cardboard sleeve. She agreed to transcribe the full contents and tell no one else what she read. She further agreed to finish the transcription in two weeks' time.

At no time did either Sheriff Otis or the agent tell her why they were interested in the journal or the farm or the O'Kelleys, but they all knew that wasn't necessary. In Oklahoma, the OSBI frequently took over the investigation of murder. Sydney suspected that, in this case, the existence of gold coins, possibly valued at two million dollars, was a very large incentive for them to be interested.

Was there a limit on how much gold one person could own? Once the two men were gone, a vague memory of such a limitation sent her to the Internet to search for that information. A quick Google search revealed that in 1933 owning gold bullion was made illegal, but that restriction was lifted in 1975. Owning as many gold coins in the amount that was supposedly hidden in the lard can was only restricted by the sheer weight of it, then.

Re-reading the account of the incident, she was reminded that the uncle deposited $5, 000 in a bank in Greer County. She set about trying to determine which bank was there at the time and, most importantly, if it still existed.

Three banks existed at that time, all in Mangum, and none still open. Most of that she confirmed in newspaper articles from the time period.

The next search was to find the names of prisoners released from McAlester in 1914 near the time of the visit at the farm. That proved more difficult. In the end, she contacted Maria Cardiel at the History Center through the link on their website and asked if it was possible to find the names. Those names might be published in the local newspaper at the time they were released as part of the area's social news. "So-and-so's son was released from prison on Friday and returned to the area." Something like that. Stymied, at least for the time being, she turned her attention to transcribing the pages of Anne O'Kelley's journal.

The surprising thing was the lack of detail in the journal of life on the farm. Anne expressed her unhappiness at being so isolated and over the children's maladies. The most she wrote about the farm itself was how much milk their one cow gave each day, the number of eggs the chickens laid, and every so often, killing a chicken for Sunday dinner.

It became clear that the reason for using the day of the week for her entries was so that she would know when it was Sunday. She insisted that Charles take them to church each week, but he didn't always accommodate her, in spite of her longing for female company. The children were taught to read and write using books Anne had brought with her. A little work on sums rounded out their education.

Was there any history, geography, or other subjects? Without knowing what books were included in the reading lessons, it was impossible to know since Anne didn't mention any of those subjects.

Did this family, if any them still lived in the state in the 1930s, move to California during the Dust Bowl days? Did they ride it out? Or did they move somewhere else before or after?

Did they know about the gold before it was taken? Or how long it was buried there?

So many questions, so many angles. The James gang and other outlaws of the period roamed the country when Ed O'Kelley was young. Most of them were gone or soon to be gone when he got out of prison in Colorado. That much gold surely came from a bank robbery or maybe a stage coach holdup. Of course, there were always people who didn't trust banks or paper money.

It wasn't often that Sydney felt overwhelmed by a research project, but in this instance, it was proving very difficult to pin down specifics, which in turn led to the questions that needed to be answered, some of which she could take care of either online or in person.

The History Center in Oklahoma City might have more information in their archives. What she needed was focus, something she hoped the journal would give her.

CHAPTER 9

The silver pickup rumbled as it headed along the interstate. It was Saw's pride and joy, bought with money he earned in El Paso a year ago. It was chosen for its color and size, which some people found menacing on the road, especially when it roared up behind a smaller car, lights blinking, sunlight reflecting from it. At the same time, it looked like many other large pickups in this part of the country. Oklahomans and Texans surely loved their trucks.

"That was a waste of time," his companion said. "Wonder what she hoped to find out there."

"Dunno. But she got more than she bargained for."

"Yeah." Aldo chuckled. "Those OSBI agents put the fear of God into her."

They watched the encounter from several miles away, using high-powered binoculars. Saw figured out the two men in the black SUV were OSBI from the license plate on the back of the vehicle. He'd had previous experience with the law on several levels in the state.

"Do you think she found anything in the house?" he asked.

"Hard to tell. There sure wasn't anything worth looking for when we got there."

They'd waited until both Sydney and the agents drove away and their dust clouds disappeared before hoofing it over to the house. By the time they got there, the sun was near the horizon. Using military-style flashlights, the kind that aren't easily seen at a distance, they'd searched the house. The mess in the house wasn't improved by their search, but they found nothing of interest.

It was so late when they finished, they parked the truck in a copse of trees up the county road and slept there. It was almost as comfortable as the cots in the rundown house. Next morning, they went into Sayre to the county clerk's office, but the clerk was of little help. They couldn't exactly ask her what the archivist looked for, and they didn't have much information to use in a search. The clerk seemed a bit suspicious since this was not the first time in the past week that someone came in asking about the O'Kelley farm.

The two men debated whether to go back out to the farm and check out the barn and hog pen more closely, but decided that doing that at night, which was the best time to go unseen, wasn't much to their liking. Since they didn't know how the agents knew about St. John's visit, it seemed like a good idea to make sure the agency didn't know about them and their own interest in the farm.

Once back in the Oklahoma City area, they contacted their boss for instructions.

"Keep an eye on that archivist. Rumor has it that she has something from the house. I want to know what's in it. And in that envelope O'Kelley sent her."

"Charles found the two men yesterday. They had the gold. He shot one. T'other got away. Charles got the gold."

The woman must have written exactly as she spoke. This particular entry was written toward the end of the journal. Sydney got to it late Friday afternoon after Doctor Berger left. He was still working on the Route 66 article about which he'd still given her no hint of his take on it. She suspected he was having difficulties with it. She would find out once the article was published and a copy was added to the many the good doctor had published before.

All of that, everything, went out of her mind when she read that Charles O'Kelley had gone after the two men and retrieved most of the gold they dug up from his hog pen. No mention of whether he knew it was there before, and not enough information yet to guess. Of course, if he did know, the question was: who buried it? She felt there was no question that it was stolen from someone. Clearly, it came as a big surprise to Anne when he came home with it in the back of the buckboard.

For years Anne had toiled in abject poverty, trying to raise three children, never knowing if there would be enough for them to eat and seeing to their education herself. If he knew about the gold all that time, and she found out he did, there would have been hell to pay.

The immediate upshot was, Anne promised to tell no one, and Charles promised they would have a better life. Eventually.

Sydney still needed to look for anything in any newspaper reporting a theft of that much in gold coin. Difficult at best, unless she got very lucky. Such a theft could have occurred anywhere in the Midwest or Southwest. In spite of the unlikelihood of finding anything, she searched online for "thirty thousand dollars in gold stolen." Shifting the terms, deleting, adding, she came up with nothing. If a year was available for the search, it might help. Or if she knew what state.

She packed up everything and went home. This being Friday, Ben would call later in the evening. and she settled in with takeout from Molly's Café. Lewis begged for what he saw as his share, but she limited him to the special cat chow and a little tuna from a can. He was making it difficult for her to keep him on his diet.

After eating, they both settled onto the old sofa with the fire blazing across the room. She picked up the narrative in the journal and enjoyed a glass of her favorite cabernet. In spite of intense interest in the words she read, Sydney grew sleepy from the warmth of the fire and the wine. She dozed off and was startled awake by the ringing of her landline.

"Good evening," Ben's voice said.

As always, the sound of his voice made her smile. She missed him when they were separated, yet she found that when they did get time together, it was all more exciting and they appreciated each other a great deal, as if it was always the first time. The old saying absence makes the heart grow fonder certainly fit their situation.

As always, they began with his recitation of his week in California. Tax season would last another couple of months. He was good at his job and at handling high-powered personalities. He rarely dropped names, and she never asked, in spite of her high-powered curiosity.

When he finished, she told him about her trip to Delhi, the O'Kelley farm, and her encounter with the OSBI agents. When she told him about Otis coming for the journal—which the sheriff didn't know about until she told him—there was a long silence on the other end.

"Ben, I know what you're thinking," she said into that silence. "It's okay. Otis gave the journal to the OSBI, told them I was very good at reading other people's writing, and they sent it back for me to transcribe for them. Everything's okay."

"This time."

"At least so far," she admitted reluctantly. "And I've learned so much from reading it."

She went on to give him the details of what she'd read, and he became engrossed in the story as much as she was, for a moment forgetting his concerns for her safety. They discussed the possibilities, given what else she knew. He offered some suggestions, and she made note of them. Talking about her research often led her to view things differently, which in turn, helped expand her research.

When they hung up, she felt guilty that discussing her work often took up much more of their time than discussing his. She certainly didn't want him to think she wasn't interested in what he did. Well, if truth be told, his work was pretty uninteresting to her. Numbers in general, taxes in particular, were boring. She tried to show interest and sometimes succeeded. What made it interesting was that Ben loved his work, and she loved him, not to be too mushy about it. He talked, she listened, loving his enthusiasm, which matched her own for her work.

She returned to the journal. In an hour, she closed it. Charles had planned to move back to Texas with the gold. Anne didn't like the idea, arguing that they had put down roots in Delhi and a farm that could do better using the money and given enough time. She settled in, after having moved several times, but he would have none of it. She suspected he was afraid someone would figure out where the money came from and they'd lose everything. That only worried her a little, if her notes were taken at face value.

For a month, they tried to sell the farm, but there were no takers. Charles sold off the hogs and chickens for enough to pay for the move south, keeping the cow for the time being. In the final two pages, Anne described the packing, leaving so much behind, and loading the rest of their possessions, the three children, and herself onto the wagon he'd gotten in trade for the buckboard. In the early dawn of a Wednesday in late 1917, they headed south, with the farm still in his name.

There was no explanation as to why she had left the journal behind, which seemed peculiar. Anne wrote in it often, her thoughts and dreams, in a few words that expressed so much. Best guess was that she feared Charles might find it. Sydney imagined Charles, angered by her description of him and their life, tossing the journal away as an unnecessary item that only added to the weight the mules would have to pull. That matched the picture in her mind of an overbearing control freak, who wanted women to stay "in their place." That might be unfair and she would be willing to change that image if more evidence was ever found.

In the meantime, one avenue of research was gone as there was no mention of where in Texas they headed. Sydney made a note to search the 1920 census records on Monday for a Charles T. O'Kelley in Texas.

CHAPTER 10

"Prisoners' names are protected by confidentiality laws. However, records older than 100 years are open due to the amount of time passed. A request for information should be sent to the email address below. Usually, the name of a prisoner should be known. However, records dating back to early last century contain few names, and a list can be made available. I hope this answers your question sufficiently."

The email from the State Prison Board came mid-morning on Monday, bore no one's name, but was exactly what Sydney wanted. Although the amount of time which had passed was less than the 100 years, she immediately sent her request, phrasing it such that her position as archivist with historical records under her care was uppermost. Knowing the ways in which government entities operated, she prepared to wait for some time to get a response.

Meanwhile, she returned her attention to processing another small collection of papers from an Oklahoman who was prominent in a northwestern county. His heirs had determined that the world was ready to learn about his political and business machinations, as they lived out of state and didn't expect anyone to care about them at this late date. Some of the papers would have provided evidence of fraud and thievery in Oklahoma's early days, most of which wouldn't be prosecutable now. Still, it made interesting reading.

She'd negotiated the accession of this collection herself since Doctor Arnold had been missing in action for over a month, with only the occasional email requesting that she keep him informed of what was going on and the even rarer phone call.

She did as he requested, but he made no comments on any of it. The deed of gift for the new collection was a set form, and if the family objected to any of the terms, they didn't say.

Arnold would be furious if he knew that she was once again involved in a murder investigation. She saw no need to tell him since he was presumably far away and involved in other things. Thinking about him, though, she remembered how in the past he'd known details of her actions from another source. A sin of omission rather than one of commission. However, he found out from someone whose identity was still a mystery.

Was that person telling him anything now? Was he or she aware of the preacher's murder or that she was doing research for the sheriff? No way to know until Arnold said something, although she was attempting to be very circumspect. The last thing she wanted was to lose the position, especially now that she was planning to buy a house in the area.

In the afternoon, having reached a saturation point in the collection, she turned back to the mystery. Having written down the coordinates of the O'Kelley farm, she searched Google using those numbers. The information she found was more than a little interesting.

Someone applied to Beckham County to purchase the land for back taxes. Because of some facts not mentioned, the application was pending. Searching further, she discovered that ownership of the land was in question. Starting in the 1970s someone paid the taxes, deducted automatically from a local bank account. Those payments stopped in 2005. After that, application was made to purchase the land, but no dates were noted.

Someone was anxious to either buy the land or the mineral rights and was trying to identify the current owner. The farm was large. There were oil wells working around it. Someone wanted the oil rights, especially now with prices high enough to make fracking technology profitable and petroleum companies richer.

Maybe it wasn't the gold coins that were at the bottom of the mystery. Maybe it was oil and the gold was a red herring.

Giving up for the day, she closed up the archives and walked to the corner to the east then turned north one block down the street to the new coffee shop. Julia was already there; her flower shop was just two doors down.

"I hear you're still working on another mystery," Julia said once Sydney joined her at the small table.

"Where'd you hear that?"

"Speculation is a way of life around here. You know that. You found the body. Otis has been in the archives. Ergo, you're helping him find information on the preacher who was saving souls at twenty degrees and who was killed across the street from your archives. Not to mention that you and I visited the cemetery in the City."

Sydney nodded and sighed. "It's all true. I wish it weren't, though. Someone with an interest in the murder could find out and I'd be in trouble again."

"True, but there's no way to keep people from talking. A lot of it is supposition, of course. But we all know everything about each other, true or not."

That wasn't exactly true in Sydney's case. She'd lived in Gansel only five years, having few dealings with most of the people in the small town. The churches were the usual social hubs, and religion wasn't her thing. She considered going on Sundays just to establish contacts.

Julia, on the other hand, had lived in Gansel for over fifteen years and attended church semi-regularly. She also met many of the town's residents through her business. Nearly every family needed flowers for funerals, weddings, birthdays, and for the church sanctuaries on Sunday. Social contacts were the lifeblood for many people. That was never the case for Sydney, which didn't mean she wasn't lonely sometimes.

"Have you heard any details?" Sydney asked her friend.

"No, not really. Lots of speculation. People wondering if you were going to get yourself killed this time."

Sydney laughed. "Has someone set the odds?"

Julia said no, then asked about Ben and told her that Paul, her truck-driving husband, was on his way to Idaho and wouldn't be back before next week. She always worried a little when he went up to that area, where militias with arsenals tried to run things, often succeeding. Such a beautiful part of the country with some very hateful people.

When they finished their coffee, Sydney invited Julia to her house for dinner. "I've got leftover chicken stroganoff that I made yesterday. It's a new recipe and makes so much."

Julia wasn't familiar with the dish, and Sydney explained it was Brazilian. She listed the ingredients and raved about how good it tasted. Having no plans for dinner, Julia agreed, and they spent the evening eating and talking. Sydney pulled out the plans for the house she hoped to have built in the spring if the weather was good. Rain delays were not uncommon that time of year.

Julia and she discussed colors and fixtures as they looked through books with bathrooms, kitchens, libraries, and great rooms. It was the library that Sydney was trying to figure out since it would be relatively small but crammed with stuff. She wanted her office to be in there, too, all built-in if possible. The size of the room and the amount of stuff she wanted to put in it weren't compatible yet.

"You may need a separate office," Julia said. "The original plans include that."

At eight-thirty the phone rang. Landlines were still common in Gansel since getting a signal for cell phones wasn't guaranteed. Service in the area was getting better, though.

"Sorry to call so late," Otis said.

Sydney looked over to Julia and mouthed his name. Julia's brow furrowed and she nodded. They both knew that the sheriff calling so late could not be a good thing.

"Have you read through the papers Patrick O'Kelley sent you?" he asked.

"I've glanced through them. I've read the newspaper articles and figured out what some of the other pieces are. For instance, there's a plat map. I don't know what area it depicts. With only the copies I made to read, it's slow going, and I've been concentrating on the journal."

"Can you get us a transcription of everything? The handwriting makes it hard to read things. I'll get the originals back."

"Sure. When do you need it?" Sydney mentally checked her

calendar.

"Soonest. The OSBI is asking for it. They recognize it will be easier with those rather than the copies."

"Okay."

Julia watched Sydney, probably looking for any indication of what the conversation was about. Sydney shrugged.

"Has something else happened?"

"A relative has shown up. Or someone saying they're a relative. She's laid claim to the farm in Delhi."

"That's interesting," Sydney said, trying not to sound too interested. "I haven't been able to find any recent information on the farm. It looks like someone has tried to find the owner so they could buy the farm. And someone was paying the taxes through a bank withdrawal."

"Remember who wants to buy it?"

"An oil company. Denton Petroleum. They're based in Wichita Falls."

"Thanks. I'll look into them. Thanks, Sydney."

"Any time, Otis."

They hung up.

"Well?" Julia said.

"The OSBI wants me to transcribe the papers the preacher sent to me. Everything but the newspaper articles, I guess."

"Have you read them?"

"The easy stuff. Some of the papers are faded or are faint copies, and the plat maps will take a bit of work to figure out."

"I figured all of that was done by now."

Sydney sighed. As much as she was interested in finding out about Patrick O'Kelley, her enthusiasm was dampened by previous events. The trip to the farm in Delhi reminded her of the terror she'd been through, the rapid heartbeat, the slight hand tremors, the difficulty thinking.

"I know I haven't shown it much, and I just realized it myself: I've been afraid. I don't understand it, especially since I've already done a ton of research. But somehow looking through the details of those papers Patrick sent is difficult to do. He died—was murdered—just a few yards from me. I found the body, then received that envelope from him. A dead man."

She shrugged, unable to come up with any other words to define how she could pursue the mystery on one hand but be terrified to read important documents on the other. Julia reached over and put her hand on Sydney's.

"Maybe you should let this one go," she said. "You've put yourself in harm's way, and your good sense is reluctant to do that again. Fear and curiosity are struggling to make sense of what you want to do and what you should do."

When Irene, her intern, was killed in the archive, Sydney took it personally. The second time, when Dr. Berger discovered the old crime, she reported and researched it since the papers were under her supervision. Her direct involvement was more personal.

In this case, there was a bizarre, movie-like element, too, like the envelope. It might as well have been labeled "Open only in the event of my death." She was drawn further into the mystery by Patrick's sending the papers to her.

"I know," was all she could say to her friend who knew her that well.

She went into her small office and found the envelope on the desk. Taking it into the kitchen, she held it out to her friend, who looked up at her.

"This is it."

Julia took it and examined the addresses. "Does Corn mean anything to you?" It was the name of the town in the cancellation stamp.

"It's a town almost due west of here. Established by German immigrants, mostly Mennonites. Farmers. Downtown looks pretty dead in the pictures on Google."

"At least there's a post office. But a small farm town probably means it would be difficult to find where he lived exactly." Julia passed the envelope back.

"We could try to find it," Sydney said.

"His house?"

"Yes."

Julia studied her friend. "Are you sure you want to pursue this?"

Sydney nodded. "Yeah, I do. I just need to shake off the case of nerves."

"Well, let's plan to see if we can find the place on Saturday. You'll need to do some research online since you're better at it than I am."

"Not until Sunday morning. And only if the weather north stays good."

"All right."

"If you don't feel right about this, we don't need to go. There's probably some vague memory or feeling."

"Something about this envelope ... Maybe it's the times when envelopes were left on my front porch and they led to my nearly being killed. Or something like that."

"It does seem very Hollywood. But those other envelopes didn't scare you."

They went on analyzing Sydney's sense of foreboding. She didn't agree with the idea that the previous encounters still frightened her, but what other explanation was there?

Early the next day, the same man from the OSBI delivered the papers. Once he left, she immediately pulled out the contents of the envelope and began working: newspaper articles, letters, a small stack of official looking papers. She re-read the note signed by Patrick O'Kelley, asking her to take care of the papers until he could come for them. It was interesting that he assumed not only that she would accept them, but she would return them to him, no questions asked.

She laid out the copies she'd made in order, intending to use them first since she could write directly on them. Some of the copies weren't very legible, making her refer to the originals as she typed out the contents and made notes. She worked through until noon without interruption. No researchers were scheduled to be in, and no one called to interrupt.

At noon, Molly's Café was crowded. Making her way to an empty table, she greeted a few people she knew and waited for Brenda to take her order. Pulling a small bound journal from her purse, she began a free-write, writing down thoughts as they came to her. She began with a question: What is it about the envelope that was so disturbing? No plan, no stopping to consider what she'd already written, she wrote whatever came to mind. Nothing of any substance came to her before Brenda arrived and she gave up. Maybe it wasn't important.

Corn actually lay slightly southwest of Gansel. It wasn't a long drive thanks to the Interstate. They arrived in the center of town, parked, and climbed out of the CR-V. Sydney stretched, then closed the car door. They headed across the street to a café with a cardboard "open" sign in the window. In some of these small towns, businesses were closing every minute. The bell above the door announced their arrival.

It was small inside. A few people sat at tables on one side and in the booths against the opposite wall. Everyone looked up and watched as Julia motioned toward a table, and they sat. A woman behind the counter smiled and said she'd be right with them. Some of the people continued to look at the strangers for another moment, then went back to their lunches and conversations.

The waitress delivered a check to one of the booths, then came to take their order. Both ordered coffee and apple pie.

"I saw the post office across the street," Sydney said. "I called yesterday to find out what was here and they said they close at one."

Julia studied the map. "I wonder why he chose some place so far from Oklahoma City or Delhi."

"Maybe he didn't want to worry about someone knowing where he lived."

"Maybe."

When the waitress came with their food and coffee, Sydney asked her about Corn. Most of the businesses on Main Street looked permanently closed, and there were few people to be seen. The woman—her name was Ingrid and it turned out she was the owner—had lived there all of her life. The café originally opened at least a decade ago, but she was probably closing in the next year or so.

"There's just no people around here anymore," she said. "I'm moving to Norman where my daughter and her family lives."

They commiserated with her about the economy and life's decisions. They agreed the coffee was good and tried the pie.

Homemade and delicious was the verdict.

As they ate, Sydney explained her change of heart as to what was behind the current goings-on.

"Oil?" Julia said. "Isn't there enough of the stuff being pumped without adding the O'Kelley farm?"

"Is there ever enough for these companies? The price is up right now, and fracking makes more of it accessible. I'm not that familiar with the oil business, but someone wants that land for drilling. I'm sure of it."

Sydney sat thinking for a moment, ignoring the last bite of pie.

"What if Patrick came to Oklahoma, looking for the gold coins so he could save the family farm?" she said. "The oil company wants to stop him so they can buy it for back taxes and begin drilling? If they find the gold first, they can keep Patrick from saving the farm and even use it to pay for the equipment."

They discussed these possibilities and finished their food and coffee. After paying and wishing Ingrid good luck, they walked across the street to the post office. The postmistress, a woman of about their own age, came to the counter and asked if she could help them. Her name tag read "Myra Ogden," the name Sydney got when she phoned.

Sydney introduced herself and Julia and explained again who she was and where she came from. She pulled the empty envelope from her purse and unfolded it.

"This was sent to me at the archives and I'm trying to find out where this Mr. O'Kelley lived."

Before she explained the circumstances for her having the envelope, the postmistress asked why she didn't try to call him. "There aren't many people here in Corn and it should be kinda easy to find the number."

"There isn't one that we could find."

"And you want to leave a note for him or something?"

"Unfortunately, Mr. O'Kelley died. We have nothing to go on, I'm afraid, and I need to locate any next of kin. If he didn't have a box, would you know where his house is located? Or did he have a P.O. Box? If so, did he give his street or home address when he rented it? I'm working with the police because he left some papers with me."

She handed the postmistress one of her business cards who read it carefully.

What Sydney said wasn't entirely true, and she felt Julia's gaze shift to her. Ms. Ogden hesitated, saying that any personal information was confidential and that some people used boxes because they didn't want anyone to know where they lived.

"Of course," Sydney said. "However, if there is no phone and someone else is living there, they might not even know he has died. I could at least leave a note, just in case. And," she added before Ms. Ogden could respond, "I can also inform the police back in Oklahoma City where he lived."

At that moment, she pulled a copy of the newspaper article from the *Edmond Sun* and showed it to the postmistress. O'Kelley's driver's license photo was included.

"Is that him?" she asked.

The woman nodded, then starting reading. She looked up abruptly. "Murdered?"

"Yes, I'm afraid so."

"That's why the police are involved?"

"Partly, yes. Plus, he was not known in the area and there was no one with him."

"Gimme a minute."

Ms. Ogden went into a room in the back and pulled open some file drawers, looked through the contents, then shut them. She did this for several minutes, finally pulling a folder out of one of the drawers and bringing it to the counter.

"He did have a box—number nineteen. Here's his application."

"Would it be possible to get a copy of that?"

The woman nodded and disappeared into the back room again. The hum of a copier filled the silence. Sydney held her breath. She was being very careful not to say anything untrue, but she knew that she was putting at least one foot across the line. She couldn't bring herself to look back at Julia who kept silent throughout.

"Here's the copy." She handed it to Sydney who looked down at it.

"How do we get to the house?"

The directions were simple: just follow main street west to the cemetery, turn right and then left at the next side road.

"Is there any mail in the box right now?"

"Only some flyer from the auto parts store."

Sydney thanked her and motioned toward her card on the counter.

"You have my card in case you think of anything else. And could you let me know if any mail comes to him? That might lead the police to any family he might have. If there's no one at the house."

She agreed to do so, and Sydney thanked her profusely. Just as she was about to shut the door behind her, Sydney thought of something else and stepped back inside.

"Has anyone else come looking for him that you know of?"

"No, not that I know of."

She thanked the postmistress again and stepped onto the sidewalk. They walked to the car in silence.

"You're taking a mighty chance," Julia said once they were inside with the doors closed.

"Someone has to."

"Yeah, but for all you know the OSBI has this place staked out just like they did the Delhi farm."

"I don't think from what Otis said, that they have any idea where he lived. If they do and came here ... well, it won't hurt if we take a look, too."

"But they've seen the envelope, just as you have."

"But no house address. And you heard Ms. Ogden say that no one has been there looking for it."

They agreed that was odd as they pulled into the street. The sun shone warmly through the windows as Sydney guided the CR-V along Main Street, down a county road beside the cemetery, then down a narrow dirt lane. The house at the end could be seen from the county road, looking almost as abandoned as the house in Delhi. A horseshoe of cedars protected it from the wind. No outbuildings could be seen, but they might be behind the house.

Dust that rose in their wake slowly settled back to the road.

The surface of the parking area in front of the house was gravel. The two of them got out of the car and looked around. It was quiet except for the sound of the wind and the calls of birds. No sound of traffic, no voices.

She walked toward the front door. Gravel crunched underfoot. The door was still in place but sat crooked in the frame. She knocked, then grabbed hold of the doorknob and pulled, then pushed. It fell inward at an awkward angle. The door frame was damaged where the door latched, and she guessed that someone used force to open it.

She pushed the door open far enough for her and Julia to get inside. Immediately, the cold made them pull their coats tighter around them. An old oil heater stood to one side in the small front room. It was cold when she put her hand on it.

What was it about an abandoned building that made it colder on the inside than it was outside? The cold from outside pushed through the door, rustling the curtains nailed above the window.

An old, green, upholstered sofa sat against the wall to the right with an off-white throw draped across it. A chair sat across from it in the corner. No ceiling light, but a floor lamp stood behind the chair, and a table lamp on a side table sat next to the sofa. A much-worn rug lay in the center of the room, its color so faded that it mostly looked grey.

Two doorways led to other parts of the house: the bedroom to the right and the kitchen to the left. Just off the kitchen was the bathroom. The fixtures were recently used but not cleaned in a very long time. The smell overall was of dust and emptiness, if the latter actually had a smell. Sydney believed it did, but others might not.

The kitchen revealed a small assortment of cooking pots cluttering the small counter on either side of the old, white, porcelain sink, inside of which sat two glasses, a coffee mug, and one plate. The refrigerator was empty; the freezer held two frozen pizzas, probably to be cooked in the oven of the old electric stove. Everything looked used and never cleaned.

Sydney made her way into the bedroom, leaving Julia to look through cabinets and drawers. The bed sheets were grimy and tossed about by someone getting out of bed. She raised a corner of the mattress, sitting on open springs. It wasn't likely that much could be hidden there since the springs were the old-fashioned kind, although a bag or envelope could be safely inserted between the two. She found neither.

An old Bible lay on the bedside table beside a lamp. She turned the switch and the lamp came to life. The electricity was still on.

She moved to the chest of drawers sitting against one wall and began pulling out drawers, revealing a few underclothes folded neatly and a pair of jeans. Everything was neat enough to make it look as if no one else had searched the place.

What might they have found? And where would Patrick have hidden something?

She stood in the middle of the room, wondering where the most likely place to hide something would be. That, of course, depended on what someone was trying to hide.

Corn was far enough from Gansel and Oklahoma City to mean that he spent quite a bit of time on the road if he went back and forth. Standing on a corner in Corn and preaching certainly wouldn't give him much of an audience but then, neither did Gansel.

She picked up the Bible and fanned the pages. It gapped opened near the back, just at the beginning of II Peter. A key was pressed into the spine as far as it would go. She looked at it for the space of several heartbeats.

She held up the key and looked it over carefully. It wasn't a house door key, nor would it fit a lock in a drawer in a chest of drawers or dresser. Nor was it a key to a safety deposit box. What then? Maybe it fit a chest or box. Or a padlock? Nothing of the sort was found in the house. Did Patrick hide more than the papers he sent to her?

What if it the key revealed the hidden gold coins? That would help confirm her theory regarding oil and the land.

She sat on the edge of the bed, contemplating the key in her hand. Finding what it opened was an impossible task. There must be a clue somewhere.

Julia came back in. "Nothing in the kitchen of any interest.

How about you? Find anything?"

Sydney held up the key.

"What do you think it might fit?" Julia said. "It's not like any key I have."

"I've no idea." She looked around the room. "It looks like no one has been here to search. It's possible that someone else knew he lived here, but it doesn't seem so."

She turned it over in the palm of her hand. "If someone searched, they would have found this, wouldn't they? I'm thinking we should leave it here. We couldn't find what it belongs to without more information, and it might be a police trap."

Julia nodded. "Best to leave it," she said.

Sydney looked up. "What if I tell Otis I found it?"

"Then you have to admit you were here."

"He will probably suspect that when I tell him where Patrick lived. If he doesn't already know about the place. He did say that he didn't know where Patrick lived, and if he didn't then the OSBI agents don't either."

"The postmistress did say no one came looking for him."

"Maybe she was told not to say if someone else came looking."

They were both thinking of the damaged door. There was no way to know when it was damaged. Sydney's own front door had been busted in more than once and showed evidence of that, even though it was months ago.

The more Sydney thought about it, the less it looked like a trap, but she played devil's advocate to convince herself. The OSBI warned her not to get in the way, but they did leave the papers with her to transcribe. Overall, her leaving the key in the Bible didn't make much sense, since someone else could find it. If she could match it to something from the papers, it could prove invaluable.

Even her powers of research might not be good enough to find out what sort of lock it fit. The police might have a better chance at that.

Sydney told Julia she was going to take it, to find out what sort of lock it fit. Then she would turn it over to Otis, whether she was successful or not. With a full confession, of course.

She inserted the key back in the Bible, put the book in her coat pocket, and went back to looking around. If only she knew what to look for, things would be easier. She studied the room, trying to imagine where something might be hidden. There were so few places.

Julia went back to the kitchen to look some more, and Sydney went back to the chest of drawers and pulled each drawer out as far as it would go without falling to the floor. The bottom one was empty, but she ran her hand around the very back and above. The next drawer held some underwear, under which she found a man's brown leather belt, two pairs of socks, and a pair of brass knuckles inside one of the socks. She hadn't noticed it before and left it where she found it. In some states those were illegal to have.

The next drawer held t-shirts, most of them white. She pressed down on them to see if anything might be hidden among them. As she'd done on the lower drawers, she felt along the back of the drawer and above it.

The top drawer held more underwear, boxer shorts in various plaids. Nothing else hidden among them, but when she ran her hand above, it contacted something. She traced its form with her fingertips, feeling paper and tape. Finding a loose corner, she carefully peeled the paper downward, then withdrew it. As suspected from the feel, it was a business-sized envelope, white, with the flap folded in.

"Sydney," Julia called from the kitchen.

"Yes." Her attention turned from the envelope to the sound of Julia's voice. Fear or excitement raised it higher than normal.

She hurried into the kitchen. Julia stood at the sink, looking down at the cupboard under it.

"What is it?"

"Down there." Julia pointed at the open space. "A gun."

"Really?"

What in the world would a preacher need with a gun? A dead preacher, murdered on the corner of her street, no less. But then, why did he have brass knuckles?

Julia moved back to give Sydney space to look under the

counter. The gun now lay on the bottom of the cupboard, sealed in a zipper plastic bag.

"Where did you find it?"

"In the box of soap powder. I picked up the box, and it seemed too heavy. I looked in before I reached in and saw the gun butt, just the very edge of it. I pulled it out to be sure what it was."

Sydney pulled white cotton gloves from her pocket, picked up the gun in its plastic cover, and looked it over. It was a Smith & Wesson, snub-nosed, .38 police special. She'd seen her late husband's often enough to recognize it. This was a surprise on several levels, not the least of which was that revolvers weren't as popular as semi-automatics.

Carefully, she wiped the bag with her gloved fingers, folded the plastic bag around the gun, and put it back in the box. In turn, she wiped the box and shook it, hoping the gun would sink into the soap powder.

She turned to see Julia watching her. "Fingerprints," she said. Julia nodded. "Anything else?" Sydney asked, looking around the room.

"There's no basement." The house sat on blocks with a crawl space underneath. "What about an attic?"

"I didn't see an entry."

They looked for an opening in the ceiling in every room but found nothing. There were no closets to check. They stepped out the back door. Nothing of interest lying about but an outbuilding that held a few rusted tools.

They walked back through the house, looked around quickly, then exited through the front door, making sure the doors were closed.

Having finished searching and finding nothing else of interest, Sydney felt like they were missing something. She shrugged, knowing that whatever else was there, they probably would never find it. The presence of the gun worried her. Leaving it there might be a bad move, especially if someone other than the police should find it, but she wanted nothing to do with it. Otis could get it after she told him about the house.

They went out to the car and were just about to get in when

a dark green Pontiac came hurtling down the lane. It slid to a stop behind the CR-V, and a young woman jumped out.

"What are you doing in my dad's house?" she shouted. She stood behind the car door, as if hoping it would protect her.

For a moment, Sydney couldn't speak. The stranger looked as if she would spook any moment and run away. Sydney held up a hand, wondering if this was the daughter Otis mentioned.

"Your father is Patrick O'Kelley?"

"What are you doing in his house?"

Julia and Sydney looked at each other, their expressions a mixture of pity and shock.

"We have some bad news ... uh ... Miss O'Kelley."

"You know where my dad is?"

"I'm afraid so, if your father is Patrick O'Kelley." The stranger nodded slightly. "Your father is dead. He died last ..."

The young woman put her hand to her mouth, her eyes wide. She jumped back into her car, but Sydney ran up to her, pulling her card from her pocket.

"Can you just take a minute? There's more you need to know."

The girl put the car in gear. The window was open, and Sydney handed her card through the opening. "Take this and call me when you're ready."

The car backed around, then turned into the lane. For a moment, Sydney thought of jumping into the CR-V and trying to follow, but the car was already disappearing down the county road.

"Well, that was a surprise," Julia said. "What now?"

"Now, I really do have to tell Otis I was here and that I met Patrick O'Kelley's daughter."

CHAPTER 11

Sheriff Otis looked about to explode. He sat quietly enough in the overstuffed chair in Sydney's living room as she finished telling him about her Saturday foray to Corn the day before, omitting Julia's presence.

"You got nothing on the girl? Not her name? Address? License number?"

"No, nothing. She must live close to there if she saw me and then came over to his place. Of course, it's possible that she was coming to see him and found us there by accident."

Otis looked down at the Bible in his hand. "Was there anything else?"

"Yes, a snub-nose, .38 police special hidden in a box of soap powder."

She wasn't ready to tell him about the envelope she found in the drawer. Yet, she must. He was so mad at her—or seemed so—that she couldn't risk his getting any madder.

"You know what you did was not only dangerous but illegal."

It was a statement, not a question. She started to remind him that the door was unlocked, but he cut her off.

"Why the OSBI couldn't find the house is anyone's guess."

Sydney thought back to the postmistress. Myra Ogden hesitated before giving them Patrick's house location. It was only when she told her that he was dead and she was working with the police, trying to find out if there were any relatives, that she gave the information. Did OSBI agents ask her the same things? Did they tell her why they wanted to know? If they only said they were trying to locate him, she might not have been willing to give them that information.

She told Otis why she thought they might have gotten no information if they went to Corn. It didn't seem likely that they didn't try since they also saw the postmark on the envelope. If they didn't find out where the house was, who broke the door? It might have been broken before, of course.

They speculated on that and other things until Otis's anger subsided. He valued her opinions and ability to find information. It wasn't likely that he didn't want her to check things out on her own, except he worried about her safety. Plus, he knew that the OSBI would not appreciate her interference, no matter how helpful she was , especially since this was the second instance in just a few days.

Reminding herself of Otis's sense of fairness, she made a decision.

"There was something else, Otis."

His eyebrows shot up, but he said nothing.

"I found an envelope taped above one of the drawers in the chest of drawers in the bedroom. I'll get it."

She got up and went into the office. The papers were folded and back in the envelope. The copies she made lay hidden in a folder in the desk drawer. She took a deep breath and went back into the living room. She handed him the envelope and sat back down on the sofa. Until she was settled, he did not take his gaze from her.

Then he looked down at the envelope, pulled the flap loose, and pulled out the papers. Three separate documents. Unfolding them one at a time, he looked each over before unfolding the next one. He said nothing as he read, but the muscles in his jaws twitched. When he finished, he looked over at her.

"He owned the O'Kelley farm," he said without expression. "There must be a deed recorded somewhere."

"I thought so but didn't find it in the county records in Sayre."

"So, someone wants the land? What for? It's never been a successful farm, at least from what we were able to find."

"No, but it's one of the few large areas without an oil well on it."

"Fracking."

"Probably."

"There's shale oil and natural gas all through that area. It could be worth a bundle."

"Or natural gas. Or both."

Otis nodded. "That's what the receipt was in the envelope he sent to you. For the taxes on the farm."

"That would be my guess. It's a terrible copy, but it seems logical that's what it is from the little I could read of it."

"Wasn't it dated two years ago?"

"Right," she said. "Which makes me think he was here to prove ownership. Maybe he needed the gold coins to do that. He must have clear ownership if he was going to sell it or the mineral rights." After a pause, she asked, "Have you gotten anything from Colorado?"

"Not so far, but the OSBI is running his records. Unless they need help, they probably won't let us know anything."

In an ongoing investigation, the agency wasn't likely to discuss anything with people outside of their own offices. Even when she finished the transcription of the papers, they wouldn't tell her anything.

That was bothersome since it meant duplication of effort. They would consider her efforts a nuisance, of course. Even Otis sometimes accepted her help with reluctance.

Regardless, she couldn't help but look for details. A desire to use her skills and knowledge, a sense of justice, but most of all a driving curiosity pushed her into doing what she could to help. It wasn't as if she went looking for crimes to solve. So far, they just dropped in her lap.

When there was no more to say, Otis got up to leave. He warned her to be careful and left. He knew she wouldn't listen if he told her to drop it.

Sydney sat for a while, considering what little she knew. After congratulating herself for keeping Julia out of it so far, she went back into the office and continued the online search for a young woman with the last name of O'Kelley. It might be useless, of course. She might be married or simply have a different name. She might not even live in Oklahoma, much less in the area of Corn. A search of the "White Pages" yielded very little.

"When can we expect to have the completed transcript?"

Sydney hesitated to name a specific date. She was checking for information based on what she found in the papers, including the newspaper articles.

"I should have them done by the end of this week," she said. "It's a bit more difficult than I thought it would be since a few of them are so blurred, I have to use a magnifying glass."

"We were assured you were very good at this type of work."

"As good as one can be. Look, some of what we have as originals are bad copies and not the easiest to read. And don't forget, I have work to do here. But," she hastened to add, "I am giving priority to these transcriptions."

"We'll be there Friday to pick everything up. Plus, any electronic copies on a thumb drive."

"Of course."

He hung up without saying goodbye. He'd given his name as Agent Corbin and she made a note of his name and the date of his call on her planner. She also made a note to have the transcriptions completed on Friday. The archives weren't going to be very busy this week. Dr. Berger would be the only researcher unless someone unexpected appeared. It was a relief that interest in the crime scene petered out. And with the OSBI pressing her for results, she would have to delay making the calls on the list from the night before.

She checked on Dr. Berger in the reading room, then returned to her computer and got back to the transcriptions. They were more than half done. She started with the copies of the newspaper articles, even though they were more or less legible. She had not planned to transcribe them, originally, but decided to include them as part of the whole. There was one on Ed O'Kelley and his death in 1904 in Oklahoma City. A picture of the grave marker was included. Another article marked the fiftieth anniversary of his death. As the killer of the man who killed Jesse James, his history did have a certain notoriety, more so in death than it seemed to have when he was alive.

She finished the articles by noon, then left for lunch. Berger left ahead of her and wasn't planning to return until Thursday. The first hour of the afternoon was spent on organizing papers in the collection currently being processed. It was important to work steadily in order to maintain continuity.

The rest of the afternoon she concentrated on the transcriptions. By closing time at five, several more pages were done. They included a copy of a detailed narrative on the gold coins being dug up in the O'Kelley's hog pen, which was similar to the one she read in the book on Oklahoma treasure hunting. In the middle of it, she stopped typing and began reading.

This account gave the name of the bank into which the five thousand dollars was deposited and the name of the uncle who deposited it. If his was the same last name as the young man who was released from prison, and who, with his friend, dug up the gold, she could identify him once she got the list from McAlester prison.

The clock chimed. It was five-thirty and she was tired. She closed up shop and went home. After feeding Lewis and having her own dinner, she dozed in front of the TV. By ten, she was in bed, nearly asleep. The phone rang.

Startled, it took a moment to realize that the sound came from the phone on the table beside her bed. Debating whether to answer it, she tried to decide if it might be something important. What if it was Ben? He would worry if she didn't answer on a Monday night. She reached over and picked up the handset.

"Ms. St. John?" a female voice asked.

"Yes?"

"This is Francine O'Kelley. I'm Patrick O'Kelley's daughter."

Sydney threw the covers aside and sat up on the side of the bed, trying to clear her head. "Yes. You're the young lady at his house Saturday."

"Yes. You have my father's papers."

"Not exactly." She shrugged into her robe, switching the handset from hand to hand.

"What does that mean?"

"The OSBI has the papers."

"Who?"

Sydney explained what the letters stood for, then explained the papers were turned over to them by her.

"Oh."

"You are talking about the ones he mailed to me, right?"

"He mailed them to you?"

"Yes, just before he was killed."

"You found him."

"Yes, I did. Do you know why he was there? I mean, was he a real preacher?"

"Yes, he was. He was in Gansel because he was hoping someone there would contact him."

"Someone he knew?"

"I don't know."

Sydney thought for a moment. Her mind was still fuzzy from sleep and being startled by the sudden awakening. She couldn't organize her thoughts clearly in order to ask the questions that were important.

"Look, could we meet for breakfast in the morning? My head will be clearer then."

"I can try."

"Are you ... is someone watching you or something?"

"I don't know. It's possible."

Sydney considered offering her spare room to the young woman, but it was possible her own house might be watched. Or whoever was watching Francine might not know about her.

"Could you meet me tonight? Someplace that's still open that serves coffee?"

Sydney almost said, "Good coffee." Instead, she thought back over the route between Corn and Gansel.

"You're in Corn?" When there was no answer, she said, "I'm just wondering what might be open between where you are and here."

After she hung up the phone, Sydney got dressed and checked the route on the Internet. She didn't fully wake up until the cold air hit her as she went out onto her porch. The sky was a pitch-black background for dozens of stars like pinpoints of ice lying against it. It all looked hard and breakable as glass.

As always, there was some traffic on I-35 as she started south. That highway was always busy, night and day. There was less on I-40 as she took the ramp west. She kept the heater on low so that she didn't get warm enough to feel sleepy. The turn-off on Exit 101, where an all-night diner and gas station sat on the north side of the Interstate, was easy to find. The restaurant was not far from the junction.

The silence during the drive was an ideal time to think. The newest information, of course, was that Francine knew about some of the papers. Did she know about all of them? That question should be answered once they talked. However, she would leave it up to the young woman to tell her what papers she knew about, or any other information she might have. If she knew about only one group of papers, the ones that arrived in the mail, there was no reason to tell her about what she didn't know. Not, yet.

Several cars sat in the parking lot. Sydney checked the time on the dashboard clock: eleven-thirty. The drive seemed long, although less than an hour had passed since she left her house.

Sydney parked and turned off the engine, then wasn't sure whether to get out or not. Was Francine already here? Would she recognize her?

Just then, an old green Pontiac pulled into the parking lot and stopped in a space out of the light from the diner. Even in the dim light, it was easy to see that it was the same as the one at O'Kelley's house. Pontiacs were fairly rare these days, and other identification marks were dents and scratches

Sydney opened the door and got out. The cold wind hit her in the face, making her gasp. Breathing in the air made her shiver. She closed the car door and locked it. At the door to the diner, she turned and saw Francine walking toward her.

Once inside and settled into a booth, Francine ordered coffee with lots of cream. Sydney hesitated, knowing that coffee could keep her awake once she got back home. Sleep really wouldn't be an option anyway. What had transpired so far, and whatever was to come, would be enough to steal sleep. She ordered coffee and doughnuts for both of them.

Sydney took off her coat and Francine settled back. The

younger woman kept her coat on, holding it together in the front with both hands. When she saw Sydney looking at her, she said, "It's so cold."

Sydney nodded. When talking about what was important was difficult, start with the weather.

"Are you in any danger?" Sydney asked.

"I don't know. Daddy thought I might be if things didn't go well." She looked down at her hands. "Things didn't go well."

"No, they didn't. Do you know who he was supposed to meet in Gansel?"

"No. I told you on the phone."

"Did it have something to do with the farm? The one in Delhi?"

"Yes. I didn't understand everything. Had to do with taxes and selling the land and all. He said something about gold once. Seemed pretty excited."

"Do you know what papers he sent me?"

The waitress came back with their coffee and doughnuts at that moment, and they fell silent. Sydney thanked her.

"If y'all need anything else, just holler."

Sydney nodded and thanked her again. "Do you know what papers he sent me?" Sydney asked again.

"I didn't know he sent 'em."

"Well, what papers did he have that you knew about?"

"There was some articles from a newspaper and maybe somethin' to do with the taxes. There might have been what he called a deed. And he mentioned something about gold, like I said."

"Did he have some gold with him?"

"You think that might be why he was killed?"

"Not exactly, but ..."

"Daddy said something about finding money to save the land. He talked to me some, but there was someone he phoned sometimes. I overheard a bit."

"Did you live with him in that house in Corn?"

"No, we lived separate. He thought I'd be safer."

Sydney figured that Francine would not tell her where she was living and decided she did not want to know anyway. If she didn't, then she couldn't tell anyone.

"There was a key," Sydney said. "It was hidden in his Bible on the bedside table."

Francine looked up with interest. She lowered her gaze and took a drink of her coffee.

"It isn't for a door or safe deposit box or anything like that. Was there a box or chest somewhere in the house?"

Francine shook her head without looking up. There was no reason the young woman should trust her, but she seemed to need to know about her father and what he was working on. The land, the gold, maybe oil on the land, all of those things were in the works. Her father was killed for all of those. She was his heir.

"Were you and your father close?"

A smile touched Francine's lips.

"I didn't know him. He and my mom broke up when I was thirteen. He moved to Colorado. When Mama died, I managed to find him and let him know. He came back three months ago, talking 'bout some scheme to get the land back. Taxes weren't paid for a while, and I got the notice 'cause they didn't know where he was."

She looked down at her hands. After a long moment, she asked, "How did he die?"

Sydney considered the question before answering. How much should she tell her? Murder was never a pleasant subject, and the murder of Patrick was brutal in its way. In the end, she described how he stood on the street corner across from the archives, preaching to no one. As she told this, it occurred to her that the choice of that site was probably dictated by his plan to meet someone. She told how she found him, that he was stabbed and left to die.

"It was so cold," she added. "I don't think he felt much." There was a short silence. "So, he knew how to get the money to pay off the taxes?"

Francine nodded.

"Did he say where the money was coming from?"

The young woman shook her head.

"Nothing was in the papers he sent me," Sydney continued.

"But he mentioned something to you."

"Something about some gold that belonged to his great-grandpa. I didn't put much stock in that."

"Why?"

"His family never amounted to much. The land was the most they ever owned."

"Did you know that the original O'Kelley owner of that farm abandoned it and moved to Texas?"

"No. Dad never told me much about his family."

Sydney concentrated on her coffee for a moment. This young woman knew little about her father's family or what was going on now or how to manage what was probably her inheritance. She needed the help of someone who knew the law and who would be willing to fight for her legacy. There were a few lawyers who might be willing to help, but none who would do work *pro bono*. The gold might be enhancement enough, if it existed.

She put her coffee cup down and looked over at Francine.

"You have no idea what that key might open? The one I found in the Bible."

The young woman shook her head, but there was a look in her eye, a hesitation. If she didn't know exactly, she could guess, Sydney was certain.

"If we can find any assets that belonged to your father, we might then be able to not only save your land but also do something with it. You need a lawyer. If the gold exists, that would be incentive enough for one to help you. If you can get clear title to the land, you can sell it. That would be additional incentive."

All she got was a blank look.

"Francine, you need someone else who can help you. I don't have knowledge of the law. I can't represent you in court or in negotiations. I have no legal standing. If you have any idea where the gold might be, you need to get help to find it. I think whatever that key fits has something to do with your father's assurances about the land."

"There really is gold somewhere?"

"Possibly."

"I don't know. Where's the key?"

"The Filmore County sheriff has it right now. He's a good man and would help you."

The drive home was dark and cold, with fewer headlights piercing the night. Sydney went over and over the conversation with Francine. She hoped she convinced the girl that finding whatever the key fit was important, if also dangerous. She might not know, but it was almost a sure bet that she knew something. Relief suddenly rushed over her, relief that the Bible and key were in Otis's hands. When the young woman asked if she could see the papers, Sydney told her they were also with the sheriff. She made no mention of the copies in her possession or that the OSBI gave her originals to transcribe.

She sure didn't want someone who might be willing to steal it thinking any of it was in her possession. That happened before. Twice. The idea of its happening again was terrifying. Sydney couldn't get rid of the feeling that something didn't quite fit, but she wasn't sure what it was. Her fear was making it difficult to think.

The concept of fear brought to mind her initial reluctance to go through the envelope she received from Patrick O'Kelley. She was reluctant to get involved again, to know why the man was murdered. How could she start all over again? Especially with papers that didn't really belong to her or the archives. Her involvement in the previous two crimes came about because of collections in the archives. The first was forced on her by the killing of her intern after the arrival of a new collection. The second occurred after Dr. Berger discovered the old, unsolved crime mentioned in another collection.

Researching, helping to solve those crimes, old ones and new ones in both instances, was exciting and dangerous. The first time, she fought for her life in her own office and for Ben's. The second time, she was left in the Crossed Timbers wilderness in the middle of winter, where she could have died. Not to mention the home invasions and car chases.

Self-preservation made her want to back away from this mystery. Neither she nor the archive was required to resolve it.

It was only a matter of a couple of months since the second case ended.

Sydney cranked up the heat. She was far from sleepy, and felt very cold. Was it fear for herself or for Francine?

CHAPTER 12

No researchers were scheduled for the day, so after her late night, Sydney arrived at the archives at noon. Once she got everything set up for the day and a cup of coffee in hand, she called the sheriff's office and left word for Otis to call her.

She forced herself to concentrate on the latest organizing project, avoiding any thought of the O'Kelleys for the first hour. She couldn't even face the transcriptions, putting the work off until the next day. Friday loomed over all, but the rest wouldn't take as much time.

It was near closing time when the front doorbell rang. Otis's big black SUV was visible from the window beside her desk. A blast of cold air preceded the sheriff's entry into the hallway. Was it ever going to be warm again? He stood aside to let her lead the way into her office. He sat in his usual chair and took off his hat. She wondered how long that chair would hold up under his weight.

"So," he said.

"Yeah. I mean, thanks for coming by."

Otis nodded.

"I got a call late last night. It was Francine, O'Kelley's daughter. She wanted to talk to me about … well … about everything. She's afraid."

"I would be, too. Did she have any helpful information?"

"Not really. She asked me about the papers that her father sent me. I don't think she knew about those hidden in his house."

"Was she looking for any specific information?"

"Not really. At least her questions seemed rather vague. I

didn't tell her much, but I did ask her about the key. She said she knew nothing about it."

"Did you tell her who has the key now?"

Sydney thought a moment. "Yes, I told her I gave it to the sheriff. I did tell her I found the key in the Bible."

He was quiet a moment. Her own thoughts rambled, touching on one fact, then another.

"Well, she knows you had it," he said.

"True. There was no way I was going to let her think I still have it."

"Let's hope she believes you don't."

He asked a few more questions about where they met. Then he asked if she knew where Francine lived.

"Not for sure. I think it must be close to her father's house since she showed up so quickly on Saturday, just as we were about to leave. and we met between there and here."

"We?"

"Me." She'd almost let it slip that Julia was with her. No one needed to know that.

Otis nodded, accepting that for the time being.

"If Francine gets in touch with you again, refer her to me. She needs to call me, Sydney. You need to let me handle things from here on."

She nodded.

"I mean it."

"I know. What if she won't talk to you, though? She's afraid and might think it's safer to talk to me."

"Then you call me. If you're meeting her, call me. If she tells you where she is, call me."

"All right."

"What about the transcriptions?"

"Nearly done. I'll finish them up by Friday. That's when I promised them."

He stood up. "I'd best get back."

She stood to follow him to the door, so she could lock it behind him.

"Oh," he said, stopping abruptly and turning around. "We're pretty certain the key goes to a storage locker somewhere. Most of them have stopped using padlocks, and the keys they use now look like this one. It'll take a while, but we should be able to find out which one. There's a code on the key."

"Good. If Patrick did find the gold, it might be in there."

"If it even exists." He opened the door and stepped out onto the sidewalk. "Let me know if the girl gets in touch with you again or anything else happens," he said.

She said she would, then watched him walk to the SUV across the street. Knowing he was on the lookout and within call in an emergency made her feel safer. Remembering the times she fought for her own life reminded her that he couldn't always be around.

The gold might be the key to the whole mystery, yet she couldn't help thinking that it might be more the means to an end. If there was oil under the Delhi farm, the value of those acres could be tremendous. It was only a guess that Patrick was trying to find the gold in order to save the farm. Did he suddenly find something about its whereabouts? Logic said that was the case since he'd only recently returned to Oklahoma.

He would want his daughter to have a secure future, so he probably planned on enlisting her help. Protecting her was his first priority, if Francine read his intentions correctly. What made him think there would be danger, though? Who or what was the initial threat?

A question suddenly popped into her head. Was Francine really his daughter? She took the word of a perfect stranger and she didn't seem to know much about his family. That in itself wasn't unusual, of course, especially if she lived with her mother after the divorce.

It was nine p.m. when she finally found the records. The forms appeared on her screen and she read them carefully. She'd accessed more than one genealogy site and the few state records that were public. Francine's mother died, so there must be a death certificate and an obituary, no matter how brief the latter might be and it was brief.

Helen O'Kelley was a poor woman of no importance to the world at large. A husband and daughter survived her.

The husband's name: Patrick. Helen died in childbirth. The daughter's name: Francine. Francine died two days after the funeral.

Sydney stared at the screen for several minutes. The young woman she met wasn't Francine O'Kelley. Who was she then? Someone who worked for one of the oil companies, one that was trying to buy the farm? Perhaps a more distant relative wanted to cash in on Patrick's finding the gold and his subsequent death?

She knew about the papers. Or did she? Did she, or whomever she worked for, guess that he might have sent the papers to her? That wasn't really very likely but it wasn't impossible that word got out somehow. Of course, her habit of getting involved could be known to them, too.

She called Otis the next day and left word with the dispatcher that she needed to talk to him about Francine. When he called back, he didn't seem terribly surprised by the revelation.

The rest of the week was uneventful, with only one researcher coming in unannounced on Thursday morning, a student from Oklahoma State University working on a thesis. The information she wanted was found quickly. Dr. Berger called to say he wouldn't be in after all.

By Friday, Sydney finished up the transcriptions and Agent Corbin picked them up mid-afternoon along with the originals. The files were deleted from her computer as the agent watched, but she'd already printed out copies of her work to go with the copies of the originals she made earlier.

The lull in activity regarding the gold and the farm made her relax. It looked as if she wasn't going to be involved much more than she already was. The fact that Francine wasn't who she said she was still nagged at her.

If the young woman called again, Sydney was determined to meet with her. Her fingerprints would help identify her, and if she could get them, Otis could find out who she really was. He wasn't surprised when Sydney told him Francine died shortly after birth. That the girl didn't know about the storage locker was one of the facts he found suspicious. Oh, she promised not to meet with her, but to call Otis instead. That would work as well. He could get the fingerprints and maybe even take Francine, or whoever she was, in for questioning.

There must be someone who knew where the storage locker was located. However, storage places were everywhere. There were two in Gansel, alone. Thank goodness someone else was working on that search.

The frustrating part at that moment, however, was that she had no idea where the official investigation stood. What did the OSBI know? Who was involved? How diligently were the OSBI and sheriff's office working on solving this murder?

You've no dog in this fight, she told herself. *Let it go.*

Her fear was diluted by the silence she hated so much. Her curiosity was heightened. She had already found information the professionals missed or didn't even look into. Or maybe she just found it first.

Friday night, she brought Ben up-to-date on what was happening. She didn't tell him that she was feeling frustrated because of the lack of feedback. He was glad that her involvement was lessening.

"I'll rest easier knowing you aren't so involved anymore," he said. "You have no idea how much I worry. I'm so far away and can't be of any help."

"You do help. I can discuss the information with you, which helps me to ..."

"I don't mean in that way. I mean if you get into trouble. If I were there, I could help protect you. If you were here, you wouldn't need any protection."

She bristled a moment at the thought of someone thinking she needed to be protected. Most of her life, she'd taken care of herself. Overall, she preferred it that way.

At the same time, she loved that he cared. When she was with him, she felt comfortable and safe. Ben was strong and gentle. She loved having him close when they were together but was more relaxed and calm when they were apart.

There was no way to tell him all of that, of course, without taking the chance of hurting him. All she knew was that her independence was very important, and it felt as if he threatened that sometimes.

Saturday was shopping day, and Sydney headed to Edmond early for groceries and a few other items on her list. Her weekend was free. Julia's husband, Paul, made it home, so she would be occupied with wifely stuff. On such weekends, Sydney often went into the office and took care of some work, or worked at home, whichever was more convenient.

As she put the groceries in the back of the CR-V, a familiar car passed by in the opposite lane of the parking lot. She stopped and watched, one hand on the hatch. With a quick, downward push, she closed the hatch and hurried to get in the car and back out. All the while, she kept an eye on the other car.

It was easy to remember: the dents and scratches, missing insignia, dark green color. What she noticed for the first time as she followed it out of the parking lot was the license plate. Not Oklahoma, but Colorado. Patrick had lived in Colorado. Francine, according to her story, lived in Oklahoma. So, was this Patrick's car or did the young woman claiming to be his daughter live in Colorado?

If it was Patrick's, how did he get it to Oklahoma along with the pickup, and why? He probably didn't bring it to give to Francine—or whatever the girl's name was—since she wasn't his daughter. The question now was, would she be shopping in Edmond if she was living in Corn? Where else she might go that was closer, she couldn't say. She followed the green Pontiac onto a main road going east. It appeared at first that she was headed for the Interstate, but she turned onto one of the roads heading north.

In the Saturday morning traffic, it was easy to stay far enough behind the green car, but easy to lose sight of it as cars moved from lane to lane, everyone driving in a hurry they wouldn't be able to explain. Edmond was a terrible town to drive in at any time, as its population was rising and the roads became more and more clogged.

The speed limit was forty-five miles-an-hour, but the green car was doing at least fifty. Two cars between them slowed her down a bit, but she managed to keep the green car in sight until it made it through a traffic light that turned red before Sydney reached it. She waited, tapping the steering wheel, willing the light to change. The green car disappeared over the next hill. Another car turned in that direction from the cross street, and when she was able to cross the intersection, it slowed her down again.

She kept straight but slowed to look right and left at two intersections before going on. As she passed a small, dilapidated, house set back from the road a bit, she saw the car parked next to a very large silver Dodge Ram pickup. Francine was walking to the door with a plastic grocery bag. Sydney, satisfied now that it really was the young woman, drove past, then turned around at the first opportunity and drove back until she could see the house from a distance. She pulled off the road and onto the dirt shoulder as far as possible and still keep the house and car in sight. She left the motor running.

The house was practically falling down with fading white paint over the wooden siding. There were probably two bedrooms, a kitchen, living room, and bathroom but each room must be small. Roofing tiles curled up on the corners, and one of the windows was covered with cardboard. The sedan was hidden by the massive pickup truck when she'd passed.

Why did people around here love trucks so much? Some people called the huge vehicles phallic symbols. The driver or passenger certainly could look down on those in smaller vehicles, and they looked ominous in rear view mirrors, especially if the driver pushed it up close to your back bumper. The headlights being that high tended to blind drivers, too. Maybe such a vehicle gave some a feeling of superiority.

That was not her problem at the moment. She would not, and could not, walk up to the door and ask if Francine was in. It might be hours before someone came or went, and she was missing the lunch she so looked forward to. She opened the glove compartment and took out the small notepad and a pen and wrote down the license number of the truck, guessing at two of the figures. The plate was muddy, and looking from that angle, it wasn't entirely clear. With a partial, plus the type of truck and color, Otis would have a good chance of determining who it belonged to. She'd seen the license number on the Pontiac as she followed it, but remembered only the first three digits. She wrote that much down, too.

She put the pad and pen back in the glove compartment. Just as she started to put the car in drive, a man came out of the house and went to the pickup. He opened the passenger door and took something out, then carried it into the house. She didn't have a clear view but it looked very much like a rifle.

As soon as he disappeared back inside, Sydney put the CR-V in gear and headed back into downtown Edmond. Except for the license numbers, she had no more information than before, only vague questions and surmises. There was too little on which to base an opinion. Hell, she didn't even know how many people there might be in that house.

The best thing to do was to tell Otis where she saw Francine and when. Let him check out the license plate number and maybe identify the man.

Saw opened the door to go back to the truck and get some papers. As he did, he saw a green CR-V drive south, past the house. He also saw the driver, recognizing her from the times he'd followed her and from Francine's description.

He waited until the vehicle was out of sight, then went on out to the truck and retrieved the papers. Back inside, he lay them on the table.

"Your archivist friend just drove by," he said.

"Sydney? Did she seem to notice you or anything?"

"Nah. I don't think she even looked this way. Why would she?"

"Odd that she would be around here," Aldo said, looking up from his soup.

"Not so much," Francine said. "Gansel is small and doesn't have much in the way of shopping. It's Saturday. She probably comes down to get groceries and stuff." She thought a moment. "Which way was she headed?"

"South."

"Then she didn't follow me from Edmond. It's just a coincidence."

"Maybe. But if I see her around here again, I'm going to get worried," Saw said.

"We've got other things to worry about," Francine said. "Mr. Franklin thinks that Sydney might have information on the key and maybe on the bank where the bulk of those gold coins were deposited. She's very good at finding information. She said the sheriff has the key now, but she may still have it."

"If the law has it, we won't be able to get to it, even if we knew what lock it fits" Saw said. Aldo looked from him to her.

"True. But they do talk, and we can find out eventually where it is and if they know what it goes to."

"You never saw it?" Saw asked.

"No, Patrick kept most of the stuff hidden away. I knew about the papers he sent to the archivist, but that was all. The guys who searched the house weren't very thorough."

"But they were neat. The house didn't look like it was searched."

"Do we know who it was?"

"Not a clue."

"Maybe it wasn't searched," Aldo said. "Maybe the door was broken another way."

They continued talking about the door and the fact that the house may or may not have actually been searched before Sydney got there.

"Whatever," Francine said. "For now, we keep an eye on the archivist and especially the archives. Something's bound to happen."

CHAPTER 13

Otis took the note with the description of the man and the house just outside of downtown Edmond and slipped it into his notebook. He particularly mentioned the license number. Crossing his legs, he shifted in the chair, which creaked under his weight. It was Sunday, and they were in her office in the archives. She felt better these days doing this sort of business outside of her home.

"So, you think the truck was new."

"It didn't have temporary tags, but yes. It looked very new. Big and silver. One of those four-door, stretched pickups and very high off the ground. They're made to look intimidating."

"A Dodge Ram."

"Yes."

"How about Francine's car? Can you remember any more of the license number?"

"No. I'm sorry. I was so surprised at seeing her in Edmond that I didn't think at first, then she got so far ahead of me with cars in between." She shrugged.

"It will be interesting to see who her car is registered to. But don't be surprised if it turns out that the tags are stolen and we won't be able to match them up."

"Understood."

He gave her a look that she remembered from several times before.

"I know. I shouldn't have followed her. But how could I not? You need to know more about her, like where to find her, and she was right there."

"I do appreciate the information, Sydney, but it's just not

safe. You've been lucky so far. And you've done good work. But you're not official. You don't have a badge. You're not trained. And bad guys won't be leery of killing you and dumping your body somewhere."

She shivered. Much of what he said was true. His words made her recall waking up in the cold of the Crossed Timbers region, where someone dumped her a couple of months earlier. Just what Otis said.

After a few more words of thanks and warning, he left. A couple of hours later, she checked out both floors of the building, making sure everything was in place. She gathered up her things and left, making doubly sure to lock the side door exiting to the gravel parking lot on that side of the building. When she reached the CR-V, she turned and looked over at the empty lot on the corner, diagonally across from the old bank building that now served as the archives.

It was nearly four weeks since she found the preacher dead near his pickup. It was so cold that day, even colder when she found him. *Saving souls at twenty degrees*, Julia had said. Except no one was there to listen.

It was warmer today, and it was beginning to look like the cold snap was ending. Everyone would be grateful for that. The whole winter was extremely cold this year, with black ice in January and freezing temperatures into March.

She opened the door of the car and climbed in. Freshly made cabbage soup waited at home, probably the last until next winter.

The screen of the laptop went blank. She sat at her desk, torn between doing more research on O'Kelleys, Francine, the bank in Mangum, and anything else she could come up with. Curiosity was still driving her toward the search; it was always a strong force in her life. How could she not find out as much as possible?

The first thing on the list was to identify any storage facilities near Corn or between there and Gansel. Patrick could have used one in Colorado or anywhere else, but he probably wanted it nearby. That was assuming that he had found the gold and hidden it away himself.

What would be most helpful? More information on the farm? Or on the gold? The chances of finding the latter were pretty remote, unless it was in the storage unit.

It was likely that whoever ended up with it in 1914 would have spent it, dispersing it over a wide area. Once more, though, the possibilities were endless. Gold spent or hidden? If hidden, where? It was buried once, and few people knew of its existence. Knowing Ed O'Kelley's history and that of the people he hung out with or admired, it was stolen. That was assuming, of course, that Ed had anything to do with it.

Ed was killed ten years before the gold was dug up. Both happened in the same state, but miles apart. What she needed was a connection of some sort between Charles and Ed, other than their last names. A connection was more possible now that she knew Charles bought the farm in 1903.

Monday started out slow and calm. The only excitement was nearly tripping over Lewis as she left the house. He yowled and ran under the bed. Sydney coaxed him out and made sure he was all right. He was a forgiving cat and was soon purring as she stroked his long body. He watched with half-closed eyes as she left.

In winter, it was always colder in the archives when she arrived on Monday mornings. The heat was turned even lower on weekends, even though she was there Sunday. Warm air wasn't especially good for papers and books, and archives were kept cool. She dressed accordingly and kept fingerless gloves in the desk drawer, a heavy sweater hanging on the coat tree, and a warm scarf to wrap around her neck. This morning she needed them all.

She began the day working on the small Taylor collection. It was almost finished in spite of the O'Kelley business taking up much of her time the past few weeks. Brent Taylor owned a ranch and a couple of businesses in and around Bartlesville. Although his family lived in the area for three generations, they had little impact on the politics and commerce during their lifetimes. They went about their business with quiet determination. All of which made their papers no different from most of the collections in the archives and of very little actual interest to researchers.

The best part at that moment was that organizing the collection was almost done. The final part was to type up the finding aid and get it up on the website.

She already knew which collection she would start next. The papers came from another family near Bartlesville, but one that had been, and still was, active in local and state politics. Collections of this sort were of greater value to researchers but required judicious handling since heirs were still alive and active in the state.

The first box of the collection was finished and shelved just before lunch time. A few things needed to be cleaned up and by the time they were finished, Sydney was ready for lunch.

It was warmer than when she got to work that morning, and she decided to walk to Molly's. Chili sounded good, but so did beef stew. With food on her mind, Sydney didn't notice the car sitting in the empty lot on the other corner, until she started across the street. It was the green sedan she was becoming familiar with. The windows were dark enough to make it impossible to see if anyone was inside, especially at that distance. She started to go back inside and call Otis, but hesitated.

If he came roaring up in his black SUV—although he rarely roared in—Francine, if she was in the car, could either drive away or refuse to talk if he took her in for questioning. She would learn then that they knew she wasn't Patrick's daughter.

She changed direction to cross the street diagonally. Up close, she realized the car was running. That became heavy with questions, so she stopped just before reaching the car. This wasn't good, and she pulled out her phone and called the sheriff's office. Otis wasn't in but Sharon said she would send Bursom to check it out.

Sydney didn't wait. She knew she should but if someone was in the car and in trouble, they might die before the deputy arrived. Warily, she approached the car on the passenger side, which was nearer. The door was locked. Nothing for it but to go around and check the driver's side.

She didn't want to, fear making her hesitate. Imagination pictured too many scenarios, none of them pleasant. She put her hand on the door handle and pulled. Just then, Bursom pulled up to the curb in one of the black SUVs. She backed away from the door before he said anything.

"The doors are locked," Sydney told him.

"How long has the car been here?"

"I've no idea. It was here when I came out for lunch."

He tried to peer inside, then dashed back to his vehicle. With the right tool, it took only a moment to unlock the door.

Francine sat behind the wheel, as still as death. Bursom reached in and felt for her carotid pulse. When he pulled away, he shook his head.

He reached back inside and turned off the key. The quiet that followed seemed ominous. Leaving the car door open, he returned to his own vehicle to call in to the office. He and Sydney stood waiting in silence. Questions swirled in her mind, none of them coalescing into coherent thoughts, the sight of the dead woman was confusing and alarming.

She concentrated. They were nowhere near to solving Patrick's death and now Francine's complicated everything. Did the young woman discover where the gold was? Or what the key opened? Or, if it was a key to a storage locker, which one? As the questions swirled, Otis arrived.

The office felt even colder as Sydney watched out the window. Across the street, a flurry of activity surrounded the green car. OSBI agents–Corbin and a woman–arrived. They and Otis's deputies watched as the EMTs got Francine's body out and onto a black body bag laid out over a stretcher. More pictures and fingerprints were taken. The evidence discussed.

Her appetite gone after the discovery of the dead woman, Sydney had returned to the archives before Otis arrived and watched from the warmth and safety of her office. Even so, she couldn't get warm in spite of all of the clothes she wore. Her thoughts were on the young woman. She still didn't know who Francine was, where she came from, or why she was involved in the whole business. Would this death bring some sort of clarity to what was going on?

Although she couldn't ignore the activity across the street, her thoughts turned inward. She didn't realize that Otis left the scene until he knocked on the front door of the building. She opened it to let him in, and they went into her office.

"There's coffee," she said.

He accepted the offer and followed her into the small break room to fix it up himself. Before knowing better, she'd assumed that he drank it black. Instead, he liked a bit of sugar and lots of cream. He stirred everything in, took a sip, then leaned back against the counter top.

She fixed herself a cup, hoping it would warm her.

"You didn't notice the car parked over there?"

"Not until I went out for lunch. I was working at the table," she pointed at it against the far wall, "not at my desk, so I couldn't see the corner through the window."

He nodded, deep in thought.

"Any idea how long she's been dead?" she asked.

"Not really. The heater was on full, which could have an effect. Obviously, though, she died this morning, after you came to work."

"How? I mean, how did she die?"

"She was stabbed."

"Like her father. I mean Patrick."

"Yeah. No idea if it was the same kind of knife until we get the autopsy report."

She looked down into her cup. It seemed that there was nothing to go on in finding the murderer. It was probable that both were committed by the same person for the same reason. The gold? The farm, or the oil that might be there, which could be bought with the gold?

"Any luck in finding the storage locker?" she asked.

"Not yet. There are hundreds in the metro."

"Yeah." She sipped her coffee. It was already growing cold. "Is there anything I should be looking for? A specific fact, or person, or …"

"I don't really want you involved any more than you have been."

"I know, you always say that. But I am involved. I might as well be looking for the right things instead of spinning my wheels."

He frowned and put the cup on the counter. Sydney was afraid he was going to leave without giving her any direction to search. But he crossed his arms across his chest.

"The fingerprints might tell us who this Francine really was. Once we know that, I'll let you know, and you can try to find out what you can about her. We'll be searching, too, but you have your own methods and sources."

"All right."

"What we need most is to find out who she's working for. Probably one of the oil companies wanting the farm, either the mineral rights or full ownership. If she's not O'Kelley's heir, who is? Oh, the car was stolen and the plates changed."

"Where?"

"Colorado."

"So that's a dead end, except knowing that's where both of them came from."

"We're not even sure of that. But it's possible."

They went back into her office and sat down, discussing what they knew and what they guessed. The scene across the street was still hectic. As she watched, the ambulance pulled away and the agents left. A wrecker arrived.

"They're taking the car away," she told Otis.

"Guess I better get back out there," he said, hefting himself out of the chair. "Be careful, Sydney, and keep me informed of anything you find out and what you might be planning to do."

"I just had a thought," she said.

He waited.

"Ed O'Kelley was buried in a pauper's grave in a cemetery in Oklahoma City. Has anyone checked out his grave? I mean has it ever been tampered with? Who has inquired about its location?"

"The dates don't jibe, if you're thinking someone might have buried the gold there instead of O'Kelley."

"But if it was disturbed at some time." She shook her head. "Never mind. It's probably not helpful."

"I'll check it out. But it's probably a dead end."

He left and she locked the door behind him. She watched

from her desk as he walked over to the opposite corner and spoke with the wrecker driver. His deputies were surrounding the lot with yellow police tape again, attached to wires that held it above the ground. As they worked, the tape fluttered in a slight breeze. That would be her view out the window for a while.

She tried to get back to work on the collection, but she couldn't concentrate. Her mind kept wandering in several directions, none of them to do with regular work. It would be best to give up and focus on something to do with the murders.

The phone rang and she moved to the desk. It was mid-morning the next day, and Sydney managed to concentrate on the current collection in spite the earlier excitement. The ringing phone killed that concentration, and she grumbled as she picked up the handset. It was Dr. Arnold.

"I just heard that a murder was committed this morning across from the building," he said without preamble. "What's going on?"

"A young woman was found dead in her car."

"Does it have anything to do with the archives?"

"Not directly."

"What does that mean?"

She explained about Patrick O'Kelley's being killed on the same lot four weeks earlier. The lot was now empty except for the yellow tape blowing in the wind. She watched it as she waited for Arnold to say something.

"Are you involved? Is the archive involved?"

There was no way to avoid telling him about the papers Patrick sent to her. They were now in the possession of the sheriff, who asked her to do a minimal amount of background research. Then she waited for the explosion.

"I don't want any involvement relating to the archives. Understood?"

"Of course."

"Eleanor is afraid that you're becoming too notorious to be good for the archives."

Ah, yes. Eleanor. The woman who knew everything about

everything. So far this winter, Sydney was blessed with silence from that quarter. She could only hope that continued.

"You can contact me through my cell phone. I won't be back in town for a while longer. Let me know what's going on."

"Of course."

He hung up before she finished speaking.

She leaned back in the chair. His cell phone. That was a laugh. Her calls always went to voice mail.

Whoever his source was, he was still getting information on the archives and perhaps anything and everything going on in Gansel. He was away so often these days, tand she wondered if the county board knew that. She kept hoping that he was contemplating another position somewhere far away.

I should be so lucky, she thought. Then again, his replacement could be much worse.

For several hours, she immersed herself in sorting out papers and setting small items of memorabilia aside. Her stomach growled; her appetite was back. The old school clock in the hall chimed three.

Taking a break, she sat gazing out the window thinking about the two murders. That empty lot would always bring memories of finding the bodies. When the phone rang, she jumped, so deep were her thoughts. She answered on the second ring.

"Sydney, it's Otis. We've identified Francine. Her real name is Doris Minter. She worked for Denton Petroleum Company headquartered in Texas. We've contacted the company to find her family."

"That's the same company name I found when I researched the back taxes on the Delhi farm."

"Yeah."

"What was her job?"

"She was an attorney, believe it or not. Her boss, Mr. Franklin, said she worked with acquiring oil leases, mineral rights and so on."

"Sounds about right. I'm guessing now that she at least met Patrick and was trying to either buy the farm or the drilling rights."

"Probably. Which means she probably didn't have anything to do with his death. That just complicated matters for her."

"Is there anything shady about the company?" she said.

"Don't know yet. We thought you might look into that for us."

"I can do that. What is the OSBI doing?"

"They're taking care of forensics, the usual stuff. They identified her pretty quickly."

"And they let you know?"

It seemed odd that the OSBI would cooperate with a local sheriff's office but with cuts in the state's budget, maybe they welcomed the help.

There wasn't much more news, and they talked only a short while. She started gathering up her things, preparing to go home, when she remembered that the mail was still in the box. It was mounted on the wall beside the front door and she stepped outside to get it. There was a full load of catalogs and flyers. No bills, as those went to the county accounting office.

She sorted through everything once she got back to her desk. Buried among the dross was an official envelope from the Department of Corrections. Inside was a list of prisoners who were released from McAllester Prison in the time frame she was interested in. Three names.

One was James Belton.

CHAPTER 14

The prisoner's last name was the same as the uncle who deposited $5,000 back in 1914. Now she had something to search for in that regard.

The phone rang again. Sydney hoped it was Otis calling back. Caller ID said, "Unidentified Caller." For a moment, she considered not answering. She was tired and wanted to go home, but she couldn't resist.

"This is Richard Franklin, Denton Oil," the voice on the other end said.

"How may I help you?"

"I understand you discovered Miz Minter's body yesterday morning."

Word got out fast. "Yes."

"She worked for us and we're trying to find out what happened. The police wouldn't give us much information. We wondered if you might be able to describe the situation."

He spoke with a Texas twang, keeping his tone friendly and warm. It actually sounded as if it wasn't his natural accent, like an actor playing a part. She wondered if his use of "we" was imperial, editorial, or if there was someone else either in the office or listening on an extension.

"I'm sorry, Mr. Franklin, but any details should come from the sheriff's office."

"We understand your reluctance. However, Miz Minter was working on a vital project, and she was in possession of proprietary information we don't want to get out. We're certain you understand."

"Yes, I do. However, that doesn't change my response. I will say, though, that I was not aware of any documents inside ... at the scene."

The silence changed on the other end, and Sydney guessed that he put his hand over the mouthpiece.

"We appreciate your telling us that. If you can't describe the scene, perhaps you have other information. Perhaps, for instance, you know where she was staying. What kind of car was she driving? When was she killed?"

"I'm afraid ..."

"What sort of town is Gansel? It must be very small."

"Yes, it is."

"What industry is located there?"

"Mostly farming, a few oil wells. We're becoming a bedroom community since we're not too far from both Oklahoma City and Stillwater."

"Both university towns, I believe."

"Yes."

"On the map, it looks rather far from both of those cities."

"A bit farther than a lot of people would want to drive daily. But some people want to live in the country, and we're going to fit that description for some time to come. Plus, the Interstate makes for quick travel."

"I'm sure it does."

It was only the second time he used "I."

"How did the archives come to be located there?" He was clearly trying to establish a relationship with her, an aura of sympathy.

"Filmore County and others north of here are very historical, as they were parts of the land runs. Ranchers, farmers, and many others located here during that time and their families are still in the area. Oklahomans are all interested in the history of their state. Well, at least many of them are. It was a real frontier."

"But the funding?"

"The County found itself with a surplus of funds a decade ago. They used that to renovate the old bank building for an archive. The bank failed in the eighties."

"Are you the first archivist?"

"No, the second. I've been here five years."

"To be perfectly honest, Miz St. John, we have no idea why Miz Minter would have been in your town. Oil doesn't seem to be that prominent there."

Sydney decided that now might be an ideal moment to try to get information for herself. He might give up a little in hopes of her telling him more.

"Was she trying to negotiate some land deals here? There aren't many ranchers or farmers willing to part with their land. Oil rights, on the other hand ..."

"We can't really divulge details of the project she was working on," he said. "Of course, her working for an oil company would give people ideas."

"Plus, her own line of work."

"True."

"Did she have any relatives in the area? Maybe she was killed for personal reasons rather than professional ones."

There was a pause before he responded. "We aren't certain. Her father may have lived in the area."

She waited for him to continue. That sounded like they knew something about Francine's cover story regarding Patrick. Was that her idea or theirs?

"How long was she in Oklahoma?"

He sidestepped that question and the follow-up ones. After she did the same with his questions, it seemed that Franklin was ready to give up for the moment.

"We appreciate your time, Miz St. John. We would very much appreciate it if you could contact us if any further information comes your way concerning this unfortunate circumstance. We would, of course, make it worth your while."

"Any donations to the archive are much appreciated. You may be hearing from me."

"Good, good. Goodbye for now."

She sat for a while after hanging up. People in high places possessed means for finding information that others didn't have. Apparently, those methods weren't working for Mr. Franklin in one direction, so he tried another. It wouldn't have been difficult to find her name as the one who found the body; several news articles were published since the murder, naming her as that person. The sheriff's office and OSBI released only a small amount of detail, citing an ongoing investigation, and reporters guessed at others.

A quick search on the Internet would turn up her affiliation with the archives and contact information. What she wondered, though, was if Franklin or the company employed other people in the area. If so, did they come before or after Francine's—or Doris's—death?

She dialed the number for Otis's office and told him about the phone call. Referring to the notes she made, she told the sheriff everything that was asked and answered on both sides of the conversation.

"Has he called your office?" she asked.

"No, but he may have contacted the OSBI. What surprises me is that it sounds like the OSBI hasn't been in touch with them to get information on her as an employee."

"Maybe they talked to someone else," she said. "I gather that Franklin is the CFO. Agents may have contacted the head of human resources, or even the office of the CEO."

"And the CEO, or whoever, would have asked the CFO what was going on since she worked in his department."

"The CEO is a woman. Carly Amador. I wonder if Franklin is worried about some facts getting to her." She had looked up the company earlier and at that moment the company's website was on her computer.

"By the way, did Franklin ask about Doris or Francine?"

"Miz Minter, actually," she said, imitating Franklin's accent.

It hadn't occurred to her at the time that the name he used was significant. Did the CFO know about the impersonation?

"I'll let you know when some details are available and you can check them on the Internet." he said after a short silence. "If you want to, that is. I don't want you thinking that you're our spy or anything."

He said this with a soft chuckle. They both knew that she would do what was needed to help solve the murders, but he kept reminding her that she was under no obligation. He would give information as much as he could as long as she was willing. He would never compromise the investigation, of course, but they were learning to work together and rely on each other's strengths.

She went to work on the computer, looking up Richard Franklin and identifying other officials at Denton Oil. She noted the names in the journal she was using for notes during the investigation. Not only was she good at ferreting out information, but she was also good at noting down data that could, and often did, prove useful and sometimes elusive. She rarely recorded everything on the computer, however, preferring to use journals and theme books.

A biography of Franklin came up and she read through it. He joined Denton Oil nearly five years earlier. At the time, the company was floundering. Nothing that meant the early demise of the company but showing that some work needed to be done to make it more profitable. The turnaround came soon after Franklin became CFO. Other items online showed that the CEO couldn't praise her financial head enough.

The wording of some of her quotes caught her attention. She sensed an intimacy that might go beyond professional.

"Richard is the quintessential executive, especially in financial matters," she was quoted as saying in a recent speech. "He may not be the only man who could pull us back from the precipice, but he was the only man who could do that so quickly. We owe him much for his diligence and dedication. I owe him much."

Maybe she was being too suspicious. It was too easy to read something into others' words, especially women.

Shaking her head, Sydney turned back to her notes on the conversation. Nothing dramatic came to her in the review, and she started again to close up and go home. More research was in store for her there, plus some of Molly's chili to take home, which she never grew tired of in cold weather.

She called and asked Julia if she was free was free for dinner, but she was busy getting tax records in order. With more people starting to move into the area, her business was growing. Not rapidly, but slowly and steadily. It was good that her friend's business was increasing, but she did miss their dinners together.

Lewis was happy to see her as always and was most

interested in the smells coming from the paper bag she carried into the kitchen. Since moving to Oklahoma, Sydney had learned to eat spicy foods, although preferring it milder than most people. Molly's chili was still just right in her mind. Once, she gave a taste to Lewis. It was an error not be repeated, she learned, when cleaning out his litter box the next time.

She fed him quickly in hopes that he wouldn't beg from her as she ate. That lasted just long enough for him to smell his food, take a bite, turn around, and come to sit beside her chair at the table.

Pieces of his dry food didn't satisfy him, either. He rubbed against her ankles and stood on his hind legs to put his forepaws on her thigh, while meowing pitifully and looked up at her with sad eyes. She resisted, trying to ignore him as she scrolled through websites. His food was meant to help him lose some weight and protect his urinary tract. She reached down every so often to scratch the top of his head. Eventually, he gave up and returned to his food dish.

As she traced Franklin's background, she began to wonder if he had seduced Amador. He was investigated several times before being hired at Denton Oil, but evidence was always too sketchy to even bring him to trial. Except once. The trial was about his professional practices, yet it was also of a more personal nature.

A woman had sued him twelve years earlier, claiming that he managed to take her company away from her. Reading both the facts and between the lines, it appeared that Franklin had seduced her. She held fifty-one percent of the stock in the company and was foolish enough to sign over nearly half of her shares to him. In the end, she held twenty-six percent and he held twenty-five percent. Eventually, he convinced three of the other board members, who each held over ten percent of the stock, to back him in a takeover. In a few years, he managed to build the company into a profitable one, then milk it dry. At least, that was what he was accused of.

Why would a businesswoman like Amador, who appeared very savvy, fall for a man with such a background? Surely both women checked him out before hiring him. Perhaps by the time they realized their mistake, they were in love. Amador might be using him to build Denton Oil back up, and planned on getting rid of him before he could do any damage. If that were the case, Sydney sincerely hoped that she knew what she was doing.

The next morning, Sydney sent all of the information she had found on Franklin to Otis by email. Afterward, she concentrated on the current collection being organized, realizing that it was nearing completion in spite of her preoccupation with the O'Kelley business.

After lunch, she spent time checking the short list of prisoners' names she'd received from the Department of Corrections. The Belton name was of most interest, of course, but she studied the other two and checked them out on the Internet. She couldn't come up with a connection, yet she felt that James was the one who had gone to the farm with one of the others, who helped dig up the gold.

Where or how had he learned about the gold? That depended on who buried it there and when. Given the timetable, the best guess was that Belton learned about the cache while in prison. Perhaps before, especially if he was the one who buried it.

There was also the question of whether or not C.T. O'Kelley knew it was buried in his hog pen before it was carried away. He must have known one or both Beltons, since he knew where to look for the gold after it was taken.

Once more, Sydney was looking at two mysteries, one from the past and one from the present. But did she really have to solve the earlier one in order to solve the current one?

She went back to the newspapers dated from 1914, when the cache was dug up, and earlier, hoping to find news of a robbery involving that large amount of gold and James Belton. With outlaws roaming the whole area of Oklahoma and surrounding states, it would take a while. The possible robbery would be her focus for a while.

It was late Friday afternoon when she found what she was looking for, or what gave all the appearances of being a story about a very large amount of stolen gold in 1882.

The attack was blamed on the James gang, but in those days,

every crime was credited to either the Jameses or Daltons. The fact that Jesse died in 1882 in Missouri made his committing this particular crime doubtful. The one thing that made it easy to blame Jesse James and his gang was Ed O'Kelley's being a huge fan of theirs, having claimed at one time that he rode with them. There was no proof that she could find of that, nor that he married one of Jesse's cousins.

The holdup was the stuff of old western movies, if the details in the article were true. Occurring in Arkansas in 1882, a train carrying gold coins was stopped, a strongbox stolen, and the gang who did it disappeared very quickly. Why the gold was in a strong box rather than a safe was a question not asked or answered in the article. It was almost as if the thieves were invited to steal it. Even so, the strong box would have weighed a great deal.

The amount stolen was said to be $50,000, but that was never verified. The lard bucket held approximately $30,000, which would have lightened the load somewhat. That left $20,000 unaccounted for.

That the gold wasn't dug up until 1917 could be explained by Jesse's death, which prevented him from retrieving it. Since the James's were known for spending a lot of money, it was doubtful that they would have held onto it for long otherwise. It also didn't make sense that they would bury it in western Oklahoma.

No matter how she looked at it, though, Sydney could not make the sequence of events totally believable. The Daltons were a bit more likely as some of the gang was still operating until about 1892, closer to the time of the events in Oklahoma, but still a stretch.

C.T. O'Kelley bought the farm in 1903, the year before Ed was killed in Oklahoma City. Was he ever involved with any of the gangs?

Sydney shook her head. The dates and events were beginning to run together. Making up a time chart would help and she set about doing that to help keep events straight.

1858 Ed O'Kelley born

1892 EO killed Bob Ford in Creede, Colorado

1900 EO released from Colorado State Prison in Canon City
1903 EO arrested in OKC by Joe Burnett
1903 C.T. O'Kelley buys farm near Delhi, Oklahoma
1904 Burnett kills EO. Interred at Fairlawn Cemetery in OKC
1917 Gold dug up in C.T.'s hog pen

Ben called at the usual time Friday evening, and Sydney and he discussed their plans to meet in San Diego, which didn't seem to be getting closer very fast. The date was favorable, at least, in the last week of April, after tax season ended and near the beginning of tornado season in Oklahoma. Since she was attending an archivist conference for several days, part of the expense was tax deductible.

He described his week and the good news was that his client list was still growing. So much so that he'd decided to hire an assistant. He expressed the hope that it might free him up to visit Gansel more often.

"When do you plan for the person to start work?"

"I hope by the end of next month. I have a couple of people in mind, one of whom I talked to today. She would have to give a month's notice where she is now."

"Someone you've known for a while?"

"Years."

"Ah, an old girlfriend," she said with a laugh.

"Well, yeah. We dated fifteen years ago or so. We never really lost touch after the breakup."

Sydney took a deep breath and let it out slowly. His next few words slipped past her.

"… married and has two kids," she heard when she calmed. "If she decides to come in with me, I want you to meet her."

"Okay."

"Look, I understand how this might not be your favorite thing to hear."

That's an understatement, she thought. *You're fifteen hundred miles away and will be working with your ex-girlfriend. Doesn't make me feel all warm and fuzzy.*

"I hope you won't be uncomfortable with this. If that's how

it works out."

"I shouldn't be." She was an adult after all.

"It might not work out if she isn't able to get out of her contract or decides not to make the move. I've put feelers out with a couple of other accountants I know just in case."

There was a silence as Sydney couldn't think of anything to say at that moment.

"I don't want you to be uncomfortable with my being so far away or anything," he said. "I'm committed to our relationship and don't plan on things changing."

"Me too. But you're right. We're so far apart, and it's difficult for both of us."

"Maybe in the future that won't be the case."

He was hinting again about her moving to California. That brought thoughts of the house she was planning to build in Gansel. Doubts returned as to whether it was a good idea if she planned to move away in the near future.

"I'll let you know as soon as a decision is reached," he said. "And if I do hire Janice, you should meet her. That might make things easier."

She started to ask if that was because Janice was ugly or fat or … Yeah, right. She was from California and probably blond and beautiful with a great figure.

With that subject exhausted, she told Ben everything that happened in her research on the O'Kelleys. So far, nothing threatening occurred, and he was optimistic that there wouldn't be anything.

Their conversations usually ran in this order, often because more happened in her life than his, as was the case now with the murder investigation. It wasn't that he or his job was boring. Things were just always pretty much the same, and there was a lot he couldn't talk about, what with client confidentiality. Not that hers was always exciting, but each day was somewhat different. She learned from the papers she organized: history, personal events, what it was like to live on a farm or ranch on the prairie. Her enthusiasm for the learning and the people whose lives informed her was contagious, something Ben admitted and seemed to enjoy.

The current research into the murder made the third time she became involved in a crime. Four times her life was endangered. Twice his was just because he happened to be visiting her. He worried when she put herself in danger in the investigations. He hoped that Otis would be around when she needed him, although more than once, she managed to take care of herself.

There were times when she did need help. Luckily, Ben or Otis or even a stranger came along and saved her. He appreciated that while she hated it. Having to be protected by someone else wasn't how she wanted to live.

For the moment, Sydney wasn't in danger because of the investigation into Patrick's and Doris's murders. No threats came by email or telephone. No attacks. Strangely enough, there were no odd emails, either, which often happened, even when there wasn't a murder.

Ben listened quietly as she told him what she'd learned so far. She expressed frustration at how slowly details were being ferreted out. He offered a few suggestions, but it was when he suggested that the financial statements of Denton Oil might be useful that she perked up.

"As a corporation, they issue an annual statement publicly. Check it out. Better yet, let me find a copy and check it. There might be something there that would be telling. If not, I could always play the investor wanting information."

"That would be wonderful. But are you sure you want to get involved? You're so busy right now with taxes and everything."

"It won't take much of my time. And it might be worthwhile. If what you suspect about Franklin is true, there might be hints in their finances."

"Thanks," she said. It was an angle she hadn't thought of.

The call waiting signal beeped as their chat turned to a discussion of plans for the weekend and what they planned to do the next week. She barely noticed the signal, more interested in Ben and future plans, and it was probably a robo call or someone selling something.

"I'm tempted to go back out to O'Kelley's house and have another look around," she said without thinking.

"I wish you wouldn't."

"I know. But I'll let Otis know I'm going."

"What about Julia?"

"She's been terribly busy herself, also with taxes. Plus, Paul will be in town."

"Go if you must but be careful."

It was ten o'clock when they hung up. She sat on the sofa holding the phone. Ben cared. He worried. On the other hand, she often felt distant, not just by miles, but emotionally. The longer they went without seeing each other, the less connected she felt. The more her life alone settled around her, increasing her comfort with that.

Shaking her head, she got up and cradled the handset of the phone on the base. The charge light came on, catching her eye, and she looked down. The message light was on.

CHAPTER 15

It was a clear, cold morning as she drove west toward Delhi. When she left a message for Otis earlier, to let him know that she was going back, she was glad that he wasn't available. There was no way she could explain what she expected to find. Frustration at having found so little so far pushed her to act. Although, she did have high hopes for Ben's finding something in the financial statements of Denton Petroleum.

In her own mind, it was certain that Franklin was out to benefit his own agenda and walk away with much of the company's assets. Everything she'd read pointed to his greed and his focus on grabbing as much as he could.

Carly Amador was more of a mystery. What little there was on the Internet gave no indication of what the woman was like. Thinking back on her conversation with Franklin, she suspected that it was she who listened in, probably sitting right next to him or across the desk.

Searching for information on the CEO was next on her list of things to do. That would wait until sometime next week.

She turned on the radio for a distraction as she drove. If she didn't take a break from the task every so often, it became an obsession. This particular project was driving her crazy because there was so little information out there.

Concentrate on the radio, she told herself. It was tuned to the classical station in Edmond. She relaxed a bit and listened to what she believed was a sonata by Chopin, although her knowledge of the genre was embarrassingly small.

Reaching the turnoff to the farm, she slowed. The house lay straight ahead, looking even more forlorn, and she chided herself for a fool's errand. She'd looked through the house before. The OSBI agents must have looked through it, since they were there the same day she was. The killers probably looked through it, too. She didn't doubt that, although there was little to indicate anyone had been there.

She parked in the same place in front of the house. The land around glowed in the mid-morning sunlight, pitted by black where small pieces of dirt, rocks, or weeds cast minute shadows.

Her cell phone rang as she climbed out of the car. Caller ID showed that it was Otis.

"Good morning, Otis," she said.

"Sydney, what do you hope to find out there?" The signal was weak, but she could make out his words.

"As I said in my message, I have no idea. Unless you or the OSBI were luckier, this investigation is going nowhere. We need a break of some kind."

"We'll find something. Without you making dumb moves."

"All right. No need to insult me."

"You know I didn't mean ..."

"Yeah, I know." She leaned against the car. "By the way, Ben is looking into Denton Oil's financials. I don't know what he might find, but it could give us something interesting. I'm pretty sure that Franklin is taking the CEO and the company for a ride to line his own pockets. That's his usual operation."

"We'll look into his past," Otis said.

Sydney was certain that he was aware of the change in direction of the conversation but chose to go along. He'd made the requisite protest over her actions and now they would discuss facts. She was glad that he didn't hound her about her security and possible foolishness, especially since her own fears and doubts kept cropping up. It was possible that this case would prove dangerous for her, but so far nothing threatening had occurred.

Except the phone call last night. The message was short, left by a woman who didn't identify herself.

"Otis, I got a phone call last night."

"From whom?" His voice was immediately tighter as he went into protective mode. In the past, phone calls preceded danger.

"I don't know. No caller ID. It was a woman's voice." She concentrated for a moment on what the woman said as Otis waited. "She said that the Delhi farm was about to be sold and I might want to look into who was buying it."

"That's all?"

"Yes."

"Any idea who is interested?"

"Several. If it's nearly a done deal, is there any record in real estate databases? Pending sales or something like that?"

"I don't know. It might depend on the area. Oklahoma County probably has such a database, but a small county like Beckham, not so much. There might be something in the county clerk's office, after the sale is finalized and papers filed. And they're closed today, so there's no way to check anything until Monday morning."

"Has Patrick O'Kelley's estate been probated?" She stepped out onto the dirt parking area.

"No, not with an ongoing investigation into his death."

"There is the tax situation. Maybe the land wasn't in his name, or it was up for grabs. I would guess that Patrick believed he could keep it in his name if he found the gold. When he found out about it or how, I can't even guess. But something prodded him to act now, maybe a deadline on paying those back taxes."

"I'll check into that," Otis said.

"Okay." She looked toward the front door of the house. "I guess I'm ready to go in."

"Be careful. Let me know when you leave."

"I will, on both counts."

They hung up, and Sydney immediately realized she forgot to ask the two questions that she kept forgetting: Had the official investigators found anyone in Colorado who knew Patrick? If so, did they know anything about his plans? She made a mental note to ask him next time, which she'd done at least twice before.

I'm getting old and forgetful, she thought, shaking her head. These days she wrote herself reminders on everything.

She pressed the lock button on the remote key for the car and approached the door of the house. Immediately, something felt different. She thought the door might be locked, but it opened when she tried it. It wasn't that something was different from the last visit. Something was missing that she expected to be there: yellow crime tape. Apparently, the OSBI didn't consider this part of the crime scene.

As before, it was cooler inside than out. The house still felt sad and empty, except for the clutter covering the floor. Leaving the door open to let in more light, she walked through the living room, then each room in turn. It was impossible to tell if anything was disturbed since her first visit. There was such a mess, comparing photos was the only way to determine that. She wished now that she'd thought of taking pictures the first time, but her exit had been hasty.

She pulled the smart phone out of her coat pocket and began snapping pictures. As she took one after the other, some details of the mess became clearer. Individual items stood out. In the living room, nothing was particularly interesting.

In the bedroom, she realized that a few photographs were mixed in with the rest of the debris. She picked them up, shaking off dust, then laid them on the kitchen counter, intending to take them with her when she left. If someone objected, the legalities could be worked out later, when she would claim that being an archivist who received papers from a member of the family that once lived there gave her an interest in the items.

After half an hour, nothing else of interest was uncovered. Disappointed, she went out the back door, closing it behind her. The outbuildings looked as sad as the house, both leaning to one side, having been pushed by the wind from the west. It seemed that either of them could be flattened by another strong Oklahoma wind.

The shed to the left was smaller with a few tools and workbench. The door was held closed by a bolt, which she slid back. Pulling the door open halfway, she looked inside, then pushed the door until it was stopped by the hinges. The open doorway was the only way for light to get inside. A few tools were rusted and covered with dust. A vise was anchored to the workbench. A scythe, some files, and a crescent wrench hung on the wall. Rust and dust covered each. There were no footprints in the dust on the floor except her own.

She pulled her phone from her jeans back pocket and tapped the flashlight app. Stepping further inside, the light shone on boards as hard and grey as iron from the dryness. As her eyes adjusted, she noticed that the gaps between a few of the boards let in slivers of light on the east side.

Looking more closely, she saw other things on the walls, some slipped into crevices between vertical and horizontal boards that stabilized the structure and provided a place to put hooks and nails for hanging things.

She pulled a wrench off a nail and immediately wished for her gloves. The surface was rough with rust and dust. Holding it gingerly between two fingers, she put it back on the nail and shone the light toward the ceiling of corrugated tin. It must get viciously hot inside during the summer. Small bits of boards lay scattered on the floor, pushed into corners and against the walls. A few nails lay on the workbench and floor, some bent, others still straight.

It was easy to imagine someone sawing boards into the needed size, nailing the boards together. Maybe even the kitchen cabinets in the house were put together in here.

She crouched down to look under the workbench, noticing a small piece of paper wedged into the mitered brace for one of the legs at the back. She reached under and grabbed it. A sound outside the door made her jerk upright.

She stood, intending to dash outside. The door swung shut. She put her hands out to keep from hitting the door with her nose. The bolt slid into place.

"Hey, I'm in here! Don't lock the door."

Pushing only moved the door an inch. She pushed hard a couple more times hoping to rock the bolt loose. Then she listened. Footsteps crunched on the ground, moving away. There might be two people or just one. It wasn't clear.

She continued shouting, but there was no response. She stepped back against the workbench and pulled out her cell phone. Otis's phone sent her directly to voicemail.

It was a bit of a hike down the track to the dirt road. Saw and Aldo walked side by side in no particular hurry. The day was cool, and the sunshine felt good on Saw's back.

"How long do you think before she's found?" Aldo asked.

"Dunno. She's got her cell phone. Might take a couple of hours for someone to get here."

Aldo pulled his own cell from his shirt pocket. "No signal right here."

"Then she better have let someone know she was comin'."

Aldo nodded and smiled. "She don't seem to plan too good."

"Good enough for the boss to be worried."

"Why not take care of her like Francine?"

Saw took off his ball cap and scratched his head, then slid it back in place. He wasn't in the habit of questioning what he was told to do, but Aldo's question was interesting. It was also too much to worry with on such a day, and he continued walking without responding. He stopped suddenly and turned toward his companion.

"We didn't brush away our footprints around the building," he said.

"Does it really matter?"

"Dunno. But the boss insisted we do that so our footprints can't be identified. You'll have to go back."

"Why me?" Aldo said. "You forgot as much as I did."

"I need to call in and tell the boss the job is done."

Saw walked on toward the truck, leaving Aldo standing with hands on hips and pouting like a child. He liked Saw. Like a brother. But sometimes he was just too damned bossy. With a huff, he turned and walked back toward the buildings, looking for a bit of brush or even the remnants of a broom.

Sydney lowered the scythe and listened. She heard right. Someone was out there, walking closer and closer, hesitating every few steps. Why? Did he intend to finish the job? Maybe set the building on fire with her in it? If she was totally quiet, would he check on her?

Standing very still, she listened as the footsteps moved around, then a brushing sound, as if he might be dragging brush up around the base of the building. She pushed the blade of the scythe back between the door and the frame and beat it against the bolt as much as she could, pushing it from inside to outside in the small space. Suddenly it broke free, the door flung open, and she stumbled.

A man's voice called out in surprise and pain as the door hit him. When she looked around the door, a rather short man stood there holding a handful of weeds with one hand and the other hand pressed against the side of his head. She pushed him hard, then ran toward her car. She tugged at the keys in her pocket as she ran. Without looking, she pressed a button on the remote, and the horn began honking. The next button, the door lock, made the horn sound again. The last button unlocked the driver's door. She held the damn thing upside down.

The footsteps closed in from behind as she jerked the door open. A hand grabbed at her elbow. She jumped into the seat before he could take hold. She slammed the door and locked it. The edge of the door clipped his arm as he tried to keep it from closing. He pounded on the window. With shaking fingers, she pushed the button on the fob and the ignition key snapped out. The man kicked the door, cursing loudly. She heard the word "saw," and thought it a strange word to be yelling.

Her hands shook, but she managed to get the key into the ignition and started the car. The man held onto the door handle and ran alongside as she backed up. His grip came free as she turned into the track, heading toward the road. As she looked ahead, a huge silver pickup pulled across the entrance to block her. It was large enough to leave little space between it and fence posts on both corners.

Without accelerating, she approached the pickup. A man, taller and heavier than the first, stepped out of the truck and stood beside the open door, daring her to hit him or the truck. She would do neither but would keep him guessing. At the last minute, she veered left and pushed down on the accelerator. The CR-V took out the fence post with the left front fender and scraped the door on the passenger's side against the rear fender of the pickup. The car rocked, sounding like a ship hitting an iceberg. On a smaller scale.

She turned right, going past the pickup. Bumping sounds came from behind. In the rearview mirror, the fencepost and some wire trailed behind. She sped away.

CHAPTER 16

Ten miles passed before Sydney stopped looking at her rear-view mirror every two seconds. So far, there was no sign of pursuit. Finding a wide, flat place beside the road, she pulled over to inspect the damage. Fence wire was hooked into the rear bumper in a way that beggared understanding. The wooden post was gone, probably lying in the road somewhere behind. It was surprising that she didn't see it come loose in the mirror.

When she tried to pull at the wire, it cut into her hands. Without heavy gloves or a pair of pliers, getting it loose would be difficult.

Hoping against hope, she opened the back hatch and grabbed the small tool box she carried. In all the years she kept it in one car or another, she'd never used anything in it. Her joy was instantaneous; sitting right on top was a pair of pliers. That joy was short-lived, however, when she tried to cut the pieces of wire. Even though there was a slot for doing that very task and she was shown how many years ago, the strength in her hands wasn't up to it.

Looking back the way she came, there was still no sign of the big truck. Feeling momentarily safe, she set to work, bending the wires so that they were close to the body of the car and not dragging on the road.

Eventually, she was satisfied with the result, especially since she was eager to get out of there. First, though, she needed to see the passenger's side of the car. Taking a deep breath, she walked around.

A long dent ran across the middle of each door. The paint was scratched on either side of the dent. When she tried to open the front door, the latch wouldn't work. Good thing she chose to let that side of the car take the punishment of scraping by the pickup. Otherwise, it would have been the driver's door that wouldn't open.

She climbed back behind the wheel and started toward home. The farther she got, the less she watched for the pickup. Otis called as she pulled into the driveway at home. She climbed out and answered the cell.

"Hi, Otis. Your timing is excellent."

"Where are you?"

"I just got home."

"What happened?" He sounded concerned. Did her voice give away so much?

"Hold on while I get inside." She locked the car and walked onto the porch. Unlocking the door, she took one last look up and down the street and went inside. Lewis appeared, greeting her and rubbing against her pants legs. She scooted him away with her foot, set the phone on speaker and took off her coat.

"Okay, I'm here," she said into the phone. As Otis asked the question again, she went into the kitchen and got out the makings for a pot of coffee.

"It was more of an adventure than I expected," she began. He listened quietly as she told what happened. "The car is a mess," she said in the end. "I don't know if the insurance will cover it or not."

"Might be time to get a new car."

"Yeah. Maybe."

"Did you recognize either of the men or the truck?"

"The tall man at the truck. He's the one I saw come out of that house, the one I followed Francine to. Same silver truck, too. I'd never seen the shorter man before."

"Did they mean to harm you or just scare you?"

"I don't know, Otis." She sighed. "There was a cell signal. If they knew that, they could have meant for me to call for help. What I saw when I came out makes me believe that the guy wasn't trying to set the shed on fire."

"What was he doing?"

"He held a bunch of weeds in his hand. If it were an old

western movie or something, I'd guess he was brushing away their tracks."

"Maybe that was it. It's getting easier to identify different shoe imprints."

The coffee maker hissed and gurgled, indicating the coffee was ready. She got up from the kitchen table and poured some into a cup. He asked if she managed to get the full license number for the truck. She admitted that she didn't even think of it.

"I want you to come in Monday and make a formal statement. We will need to find these men and question them. We'll check that house you found, of course, but my guess is they've skedaddled."

"Okay."

"If you see either of them, or someone starts prowling around your house, you call. Got that?"

"Yes, sir. I got that."

They said their goodbyes, and Sydney took her coffee into the bedroom, setting it on the nightstand. She sat on the edge of the bed to take her shoes off. Lewis jumped up beside her and started rubbing against her arm. She scratched his head and ears as she thought about what Otis said. Since the front door was broken into several times last year by people looking for things or threatening her his warning was important. She didn't want any more of it. The new house was part of the reaction and hopefully the solution. Ben wanted to be part of the solution, too.

She shook her head, sloughing off the fears for the moment, and got undressed. Emptying the pockets of her jeans, she pulled out the folded piece of paper she found under the work table. In all the excitement, she forgot about it. She unfolded it but couldn't read it in the darker room. Putting on her robe, she took it into the kitchen and spread it out on the table.

The writing was in pencil, and the wrinkles blurred the writing. It was a withdrawal slip. From the Bank of Commerce in Sayre, in the amount of twenty thousand in gold.

Showered and with both Lewis and herself fed, Sydney went

to her laptop and began searching. No Bank of Commerce still operated in Sayre. Although little information on the old bank was readily available on the Internet, through persistence, Sydney determined that it wasn't sold and had kept operating in the same town under another name. It was one of the banks that failed during the Great Depression. That failure was not a factor in her mystery, though, as the gold was withdrawn on October 20, 1915, by C.T. O'Kelley himself.

If it was really him, he had come back from Texas about a year after moving. Was it a quick trip to get his money? Or did he move back to the area? The really curious question was, why was the slip hidden in the work shed? Maybe Anne, his wife, didn't know about the gold. Being afraid to spend money was one curse of having gotten it illegally.

Finding the slip brought up more questions than it answered: Did the bank always have that much gold on hand? Had C.T. deposited it intact somehow? Sydney was certain there was no such thing as safe deposit boxes in the early 1900s but she could be wrong. Even if she was, though, a withdrawal slip wouldn't be needed to remove something from a box.

By and large, none of that mattered. The burning question: Where did C.T. put the gold afterward?

It was looking more and more as if Patrick came back to Oklahoma to find that gold. He got hold of information, whether accidentally or because he searched for it. If he did, it would have been in Colorado.

Sydney looked at the clock. It was Saturday night and very late. Tomorrow would do for checking out Canon City, Colorado, where Patrick had lived. The state prison was located there, which couldn't be a coincidence.

On Monday, the weather was beautiful. The temperature rose to a balmy forty-five degrees, and people in town looked more cheerful. They'd suffered through several weeks of cold and gloom so the break was welcomed by everyone.

Desideria called mid-morning to discuss how they would proceed on the new house. They set a meeting with the credit union to discuss a mortgage and scheduled a meeting with the builder. For the moment, plans were tentative until the realtor talked with the others involved.

Sydney suddenly felt wary of the whole thing. She wasn't so sure about this move. Maybe she never was sure. Something needed to be done, and a new, more secure house was the best option. Even if she built the house then moved to California, that would mean two rentals for income, and she wouldn't be dependent on Ben's income. The possibility of having no job, maybe unable to find a job, and having only financial support from Ben was not going to happen. The two rental properties would provide income of her own. If a job came along, so much the better.

Looking at a new house as an investment calmed her anxiety, and she began looking forward to the process and final result. The house in Norman was a new build already completed when she bought it, so the design and choices of various things were pretty much made before she came along. There were a few things she wanted different, which the current builder was willing to do. Having toured the model homes with Desideria, she knew what she wanted. Well, as much as anyone did at this stage.

She would call Ben that evening and let him know the plan for a new house was proceeding. Whether she would tell him about her weekend, she wasn't sure.

The day passed slowly, with no researchers and no phone calls or emails requesting information. Sometimes, a good part of her job was finding information for people living at a distance. Charges for copying and mailing were minimal. People looking for family histories, both genealogists and individuals researching for themselves, were the bulk of these. One thing that made this interesting for Sydney was where the queries came from, which included all parts of the country and a few from Europe. A lot of Europeans who couldn't visit the states were fascinated with western history.

After lunch at Molly's, she found herself distracted and without energy. Was it a touch of spring fever? She wanted to be outside enjoying the new warmth. Doing what? She didn't do much gardening or hiking but the air was warm and clear and so inviting.

After work, she sat wrapped in coat and scarf on her back porch with a cup of coffee and nothing else but her thoughts. Her mind wandered, the birds sang, and within half an hour, the sun was going down and the air cooling. The seasons were unpredictable and kept people on their toes, but it was times like this when she loved living in Oklahoma. After the long, cold winter, the warmer days gave a sense of relief that was so welcome.

As she came out of her reverie, she realized her thoughts had turned to the current mystery. The one assumption that bothered her was that Richard Franklin was using Carly Amador for his own gain. Although, it could be the other way around.

Too often people think of women as victims. She shouldn't be one who did.

"I checked out Denton Oil today," Ben said that evening when she called.

It was seven o'clock, and he was eager to share his news. Sydney felt her excitement rise with his.

"The company has always been considered a little shady, it seems. It's been especially bad since Carly Amador took over from her grandfather nine years ago."

"Yes, I saw he stepped down and she took over."

"He didn't step down. She forced him out."

"How did she manage that?"

"She got the other board members to vote against him."

That was the same thing Franklin did in his earlier position.

"She promised to bring the company back to good financial health," Ben continued. "She managed that, but like most CEOs, it wasn't enough. She keeps pushing for more growth. One of the things they've done under her leadership ... well, let's just call it creative land buying or leasing. It's gotten especially notorious since Franklin became CFO."

"Anything illegal?" she asked.

"Not quite, although Carly was accused by some of her victims."

"Maybe the same thing she was trying to do to O'Kelley. But he wouldn't sell."

"Could be. The question is, though, whether he was trying to save the farm for himself by finding the gold or trying to establish clear ownership of the farm so he could sell to Denton."

"I'm still thinking he was about the gold, either way. Since Francine wasn't his daughter, killing him actually makes no sense. It will take years to settle the property ownership. Unless Denton has some way to hurry it along."

"If what I found about the oil fields in that part of Oklahoma is true, it certainly could be about the mineral rights. There have been a few good strikes around the O'Kelley farm, and prospects are good for that land, too."

"Was Francine pretending to be his daughter to inherit the land?" Sydney shook her head. "Just saying she was his daughter wouldn't work, of course. Killing her makes even less sense than killing Patrick."

"Well, let's think on it a bit," Ben said. "I do believe that the people at Denton are behind all of this. They want that farm for the oil. Denton Oil picked up the rights on several small farms around O'Kelley's, but they haven't started drilling yet. You found that they'd been checking on the tax situation."

"I doubt that they care about the gold," she said. "They might not even know about it, unless Francine told them."

"About that. The company has spent so much on acquisitions that they have little cash. They've borrowed a great deal and have little room to borrow more for additional equipment."

"So, the gold would help them do that."

That last bit of information gave her some ideas, and her thoughts began tumbling over each other. They discussed it all a while longer.

Eventually, to change the subject, Sydney asked him about his plans for the week. He was still very busy with his clients' tax returns and making time to look into the finances of Denton Oil was a welcome distraction. Then he asked how her weekend went, and she told him everything that happened at the farm. Keeping him in the dark just wasn't right. When she finished, he was silent for the space of several heartbeats.

"I know you're worried," she said. "It scared me, I have to say, but I did learn some things."

"As long as we're so far apart, I'm going to worry," he said. "Especially when this sort of thing happens. You could get yourself killed or hurt."

"Yes," she said, "but I didn't. I can't help that these things happen around me. I need to feel that I can be useful in the investigation when it touches on my work or my life."

"Yeah. Well." Another silence stretched out. Finally, Ben said, "I love you and I worry."

"I know. I don't mean to worry you. And I do get scared sometimes, even though I try to be careful."

"I know. We'll talk more about it."

"Every time we call each other, I'm sure."

"Yeah." He chuckled. "I admire your independent spirit. I won't try to change you."

"Thanks."

They promised to talk again on Friday evening, expressed love for each other, and said good night. Sydney sat quietly, thinking about Ben, the house, and the things happening in her life. She often worried about the danger she might be in, but once she got involved, she couldn't back away. It wasn't as if her work wasn't satisfying. She loved learning about the lives and history of the people and land. If the mysteries didn't occur around her, she would never get involved. Why would she?

Images of the farm and the shed came to mind. That led to thinking of the two men who locked her in the work shed. Did they want to kill her? Delay her? Frighten her?

Whatever their motives were, they frightened her. They accomplished that much.

She went into the bedroom and took the pistol from the drawer of the bedside table. From now on, she would carry it with her, legal or not.

CHAPTER 17

Closing the Word file on her computer, Sydney sighed with relief. The last word in Patrick's papers was checked. The OSBI didn't really need any of the corrections she made and she didn't plan on letting them know she had made them.

She'd learned quite a bit about the O'Kelleys' lives and deaths in Oklahoma in the early 1900s. Transcribing the documents embedded the data in her mind until the day she no longer needed it. Then, it would be mentally filed away awaiting the moment she might need it again.

She took the bank withdrawal slip to the copier to make herself a copy. She was slow in putting down the cover, and when the light under the glass came on, she saw something on the back of the paper that was not visible otherwise. In fact, the marks at first appeared to be due to folding and age and being exposed to light and dust, rather than deliberate notations.

She tried to bring out the marks by copying the back of the paper, but it wouldn't reproduce well, no matter which settings she used.

Grabbing it up, she rushed down to the processing room, and looked through cupboard after cupboard, finally finding the object of her search. The light box was small, but heavy for its size. She moved it to one of the tables and plugged it in. Hoping that it still worked, she turned on the switch, and the light glowed behind the glass.

The marks were faint when she set it on the lighted glass, but they were deliberately made. It was tempting to get a pencil and retrace them, but that wasn't what an archivist could ever do. She got a piece of tracing paper, but the marks didn't show through clearly enough. As a last resort, she placed a piece of Mylar film over the piece of paper. Perfect. She taped it on the corners to keep it from slipping

Several types of pens and pencils were available, but which one would work best on the Mylar? The tip of a grease pencil was too broad. Regular pencils and colored pencils wouldn't make a mark at all. She finally found a blue fine-point Sharpie.

Tracing over the lines, she held her breath, trying to keep the lines as true as possible. It was nearly done when she realized the total picture was familiar. Taking a deep breath to calm herself, she finished the drawing and lifted it off the light board and turned it off. Carefully, she peeled the tape off of the corners.

Upstairs in the office, she pulled out the copies of Patrick's original papers and searched through them. She placed the one she wanted flat on her desk and laid the Mylar copy over it. Other than the difference in size, it was a perfect match except for one detail.

A circle marked a spot near the house on the Mylar copy. The diagram was of the farm in Corn, and the house was the one in which Patrick had lived.

She wondered why he picked that particular piece of property since discovering its existence. Now she thought she knew. What she held was a treasure map and the circle showed where the gold was hidden.

Or was once hidden.

There was no way of knowing whether the gold was still there. But instinct told her it was.

If she was right, she needed to go back to Corn but not alone. She called Otis.

"The sheriff is out for a few days at a conference," Sharon said. "Is it important, Sydney?"

"Yes, it is. But I think I can handle it on my own."

"The sheriff asked me to tell you, if you called, that you weren't to do anything without his knowing."

Ben will be glad to hear that, Sydney thought.

"Okay. If you can, call him and let him know that I'm going out to the farm in Corn and have another look around. Tell him, also, that I will be careful."

"Yeah, I can get hold of him. Will you wait until then?"

"No, I want to get there before noon. He has my cell number if he wants to call me."

"Are you sure? He might not like you going out there on your own."

"If I don't go, we could lose everything," Thinking of the gun in her purse, Sydney added, "I'll be very careful."

She said goodbye, then called Charlene to come in for the afternoon. As usual, her part-time helper was available. She also had her own key, so Sydney didn't have to wait for her to get there.

She took the extra precaution of placing the copies of Patrick's papers in the vault, along with the original withdrawal slip. She stuck a note on the outside for the envelope to be given to Otis, just in case something happened to her.

She shook her head. She was becoming paranoid, not only by fearing that someone might take the papers, but also by thinking that Doctor Arnold always seemed to know what was going on in the archives when he was out of town. For now, she didn't want anyone to give him any information about the O'Kelleys or what she was doing.

By ten-thirty, she was on her way to Corn. As she drove, she tried to picture the land around the house. Was there a marker of some kind where she believed the gold was buried? Would she have to dig? There was a shovel in the shed if she needed it.

She also kept an eye on the rearview mirror, hoping that the silver pickup wouldn't suddenly appear.

The wind blew strongly by the time she pulled up in front of the house. The gusts rocked the old CR-V, which was smaller than most SUVs. She slipped her phone and the gun into her coat pockets along with the keys. Wearing jeans was a good idea, but she could have worn a warmer coat. The door was locked. Probably the OSBI agents had either found a key or gotten one made, yet there still wasn't any crime scene tape.

Walking around the house, she held up the Mylar diagram, but the wind tried to tear it from her hands. She retreated to the back wall of the house, where the wind was partially blocked, and pressed the diagram against the siding. The grey boards were light enough for the blue marks she had made to stand out. The circle indicated a spot to the left, just beyond the work shed.

Before moving to the spot, she checked in front of the house to make sure no one was around. The wind would blow away the sound of a vehicle pulling up to the house or even driving down the road, so she needed to stay alert.

Satisfied that she was safe for the moment, she went back to the shed, where she held the diagram against the wall to get her bearings again. The spot was on the other side of the shed, about twelve yards if she estimated the distance correctly. She rolled up the Mylar and stuck it in her pocket, pulling the jacket down to cover it. In the shed, she found the shovel and tested the strength of the handle. It was still solid.

The wind was still blowing, maybe even harder, and since she couldn't hear any vehicle that might drive up, she kept checking the road on the other side of the house. She also checked again for the pistol she had slipped into the jacket pocket. It was a small .32 semi-automatic bought several months earlier to replace the one that Julia lent her. She hoped to never use it, but it made her feel that, given recent events, she could protect herself. Alone in the middle of nowhere, it helped her feel safer.

Using the shovel like a walking stick, with the blade up, she stepped off what was about twelve yards. She picked up two rocks and set them one on top of the other to mark her starting point. She took fifteen steps farther, scanning the ground, and placed two more rocks. Finding nothing unusual, she turned left, coming around to the first rocks in a semi-circle. From there, she continued around to the second rocks. She walked over every inch of that circle she formed and found nothing.

She leaned on the shovel, blade down, and studied the ground. There must be something to indicate where the gold was buried. If it was buried.

This is stupid. I need a back hoe or something to find it.

What she needed was a metal detector. There must be places to rent them. She should get one and come back. But the sense of urgency that made her come out to Corn now still nagged at her. She couldn't shake it.

Her phone rang, and she jumped, startled out of her reverie.

"Sydney, it's Otis."

"Hey."

"What the hell are you doing out there?"

"I found something ..."

"You promised you wouldn't go off half-cocked."

Sydney didn't remember saying that, at least not exactly. She listened as he scolded her more. He sounded really angry this time. When he ran out of angry words, she said, "Otis, I have my gun, and no one followed me."

"You have a gun?"

"Yes, of course."

A sound, as if the wind was blowing fifty miles an hour and whirling around drowned out his response. It nearly knocked her off her feet. Looking up, she realized it was the sound of a motor and rotating blades from above. With the sound of the wind all around her, she didn't hear the helicopter approach and was totally caught by surprise.

"There's a helicopter landing," she yelled into the phone.

"A what?"

"A helicopter."

"Who is it?"

"Don't know yet. I'd bet it's from Denton Oil, though."

"Keep the line open."

She agreed and calculated where the chopper was going to land. It was far enough away that she wouldn't be crushed, but the downdraft was too much. She backed away, kicking over the first two rocks in the process. No need in giving anyone ideas about what she was looking for or where.

The sun reflected off the glass of the chopper, so there was no way to see who was inside. Probably no one she would recognize, although there were pictures of the officers of the oil company on their website.

She tried to smooth down her short hair once the chopper settled and the engine was silenced. The door opened and a man stepped out. She half expected one of the two men who trapped her in the shed, but this man was well-dressed, more of an executive type. He closed the door and looked around until his gaze came to her. He walked straight toward her, stopping a few feet from her.

"Sydney St. John?"

"Yes." They were both shouting to be heard above the wind.

"I'm Richard Franklin."

"I know."

"You're trespassing."

"Oh? Who owns the land?"

"Denton Oil Company."

"Since when?"

"The sale is being processed."

"So, you haven't taken possession of it yet."

"Within the next few days."

"I see. From whom are you buying it?"

"That's none of your concern."

"I'm sure it's of concern to the people who still own it."

Franklin sighed dramatically. "Ms. St. John, we must ask you to leave."

"Did Patrick O'Kelley own it?"

"No."

"Did Charles O'Kelley own it?"

"If you don't leave, I will have to call the police and have you removed."

"You do realize that I've seen Patrick's papers and Charles's, including deeds to properties."

"That's neither here nor there," Franklin said after a pause. "If you won't leave on your own, we will escort you off the property."

He motioned to someone in the chopper. The door opened, and the tall man she'd seen before got out and headed toward them. Franklin kept his eye on Sydney until the man reached him.

"Saw, give Ms. St. John a lift in the helicopter and drop her off wherever she wishes." So, that was the big man's name, not just a random word shouted by his companion the other day.

Saw nodded and started toward her. It was her first clear look at him. He was taller than Otis and nearly as big. If he grabbed hold of her, she wouldn't be able to get away. There was no mistaking their intentions. She didn't much care for the phrase, "drop her off," and took two steps backward, drawing the pistol from her coat pocket at the same time.

"I'd rather not," she said.

The man stopped advancing, gave her a long look and stepped forward again. She fired. Dirt flew up where the bullet hit the ground.

"The next shot will be closer," she said. "I won't miss."

It was his turn to take two steps back. Saw blocked her view of Franklin. The wind from the blades still buffeted her and nearly swept her from her feet. She stepped farther back. Saw pulled his baseball cap down lower on his head.

She remembered her cell phone that she put in the same pocket when she pulled out the gun. She glanced at the screen, but the light was such that she couldn't read it.

Saw took a step toward her, but she stretched her arm out with the gun, and he stopped.

"Otis, please hear me. Franklin and a man named Saw. They want to take me for a helicopter ride."

If Otis responded, she couldn't hear him. It was quite possible that he hung up or the call was lost. Reception in the area was not the greatest.

The two men didn't know, either. They saw her with the phone in her hand when they arrived. They saw her speaking into it now. There was no way they could know whether the party on the other end was still there, or what she might have told them. Given the wind it was unlikely that the person on the other end, if still there, could now hear anything.

All of this ran through her mind. Would they err on the side of caution, or take her for that ride after all?

They hesitated. If something happened to her now, there might be a witness of sorts. Could they or would they take that chance?

Franklin motioned with his hand and the chopper cut off. The door opened and a woman climbed out. The rotors slowed over her head as the newcomer walked toward the tableau. When she stood beside Franklin, she put her hands on her hips and confronted him.

"What's the holdup?" she asked.

Sydney recognized Carly Amador.

CHAPTER 18

Otis wanted to throw the cell phone to the floor but restrained himself. He heard the whoosh, whoosh rhythm of the rotors of a helicopter, then contact was lost. What the hell kind of trouble was she in now? He tried calling her back, but there was no response.

He contacted his office and told Sharon to dispatch Kent to the farm in Corn. Then he called the OSBI, asked for agent Cooper, and told him what he'd heard on the phone.

"She may be in danger. I don't know for sure, but ..." He left the thought hanging.

"I can get out there, but it will take me a while," Cooper said, without being asked.

Otis thanked his lucky stars that the agent grasped the situation and was willing to jump right in.

"My deputy, Kent, should be on his way now. But it's a bit of a drive for him, too."

"We can't spare a chopper right now," Cooper said, anticipating his next request.

"All right. Get out there as quick as you can. I'll be right behind you. I'm guessing you know where the farm is."

Cooper confirmed that he'd been there and that he was on his way to Corn. Otis let the organizer of the seminar know that there was a problem and he had to leave. With lights flashing and sirens blaring, three vehicles headed west to Corn.

"Why hasn't she left?"

Franklin looked at his boss then at Sydney. He shrugged,

held Carly's elbow and turned her away. Sydney expected that he was telling her about the phone and that she carried a gun. Carly looked over her shoulder, probably to confirm the presence of the gun. Her eyes narrowed further as the two continued their discussion. Sydney felt foolish all of a sudden. They were discussing what to do, she was standing there with a gun, and Saw stood nearly equidistant between them, glaring at her.

"I'm leaving now," she called out.

Saw started, then turned to his employers. They both looked around and, seeming to have discussed enough, walked back toward her. Franklin spoke to Saw, who turned and walked back to the chopper with him. Carly moved closer to Sydney.

"I don't know what those two said to frighten you so much," she said. "We aren't here to threaten you in any way."

"I'm not sure they got the message," Sydney said, motioning toward the men's retreating backs.

"They're men. What else can I say?"

"I guess I'll be leaving now."

"Let's talk. I don't want you leaving with a bad impression of us."

"Later. Call me. Right now, I need to get home. I need to explain to Sheriff Otis what happened."

"He's the one you were on the phone with?"

"Yes."

Carly looked over her shoulder at the helicopter. When she turned back to Sydney, her expression was grim. "Those two have a lot to answer for." She put her hands in the pockets of her coat and shrugged.

Sydney dropped her hand so that the gun was pointing toward the ground.

"Even so, it looks to me like you're the one who's threatening," Carly said. "Maybe we should bring charges."

"Maybe you should. For the moment, I'm done here."

Sydney walked backward until she reached the shed. She leaned the shovel against the wall. Getting around it to shield her from the chopper, she turned and ran to her car. Once inside, she speed-dialed Otis's number as she started the car and put it in gear.

"Sydney. Are you okay?"

"So far. I'm starting home."

"I'm on my way. Me and two other cars."

She looked in the rearview mirror as the chopper lifted off.

"I'm not sure what to do right now," she said. She told him the chopper was moving away. As quickly as possible, she described everything that had happened, while driving with one hand. She headed toward the Interstate. More than ever, she wished the car was equipped with Bluetooth.

If only she'd checked out alternate routes. Even if the chopper didn't follow immediately, they would assume she would head straight for Oklahoma City on the Interstate. If there was another route, she could have fooled them. Then maybe not. The land in the area was flat and nearly featureless.

"They just might have you charged with assault since you pulled the gun on them," Otis was saying. His words were breaking up, but she got the sense of it.

"Yeah. It would be three against one in court."

"Not to mention that you actually fired the gun." More breaking up.

"I'm guessing you didn't hear any of the conversation with Franklin."

"Not a word. I lost contact …"

Otis said something about contacting Cooper and Kent to stand down. She thought he said he was still heading for Corn, but the connection was lost. At least she was able to concentrate on her driving.

A shadow passed over her, and suddenly the chopper was low and in front of her. It turned to face her, lowered to the road. She swerved to avoid a collision, going off the gravel shoulder. Jerking the wheel, she pulled back onto the road, straining to see the chopper.

It came at her from the side this time. Again, she jerked the wheel, nearly going off the road on the other side. With only two lanes and a bit of a drop-off on both sides, there wasn't much room to maneuver. Would they actually hit her with the skids? It seemed they were even more desperate to stop her than she'd guessed. What did they think she knew?

Gunning the motor, she sped forward. The chopper appeared ahead of her. Instead of swerving, she slammed on the brakes, forcing the chopper to lift to get over her. The downdraft shook the CR-V as she accelerated. The next pass was even lower, headed straight toward her from a longer distance. As they closed, Sydney could see Franklin sitting next to Carly. She was piloting the chopper.

Sydney was forced to swerve. The right front tire dropped off the pavement, jerking the wheel even more to the right. It dropped down onto the sandy surface below, sliding downward. She fought the wheel, trying to bring the vehicle under control. She managed to straighten it out and come to a complete stop while she caught her breath and looked over the situation.

To get back on the pavement, she would have to drive farther down. The bank was too high here, and she didn't want to go backwards. Easing the accelerator down, she moved forward with the back tires spinning, catching, spinning. Sand and dust filled the air behind and around her. If the chopper came toward her right then, she wouldn't see it before it was on her.

Another flurry of dust and sand rose around her, further obscuring her view. The chopper was close, but she couldn't tell exactly where.

As calmly as she could, she continued driving toward the spot where she thought she could get back on the road. There was only an occasional glimpse through the screen of dust. The pursuers hovered above, deliberately obscuring her ability to see.

Her knuckles were white as she gripped the steering wheel. Her breathing was too fast, and she tried to slow it. Her heart pounded against her breastbone. For an instant, the absurdity of the moment brought a smile. She'd seen too many similar chases in movies and on TV. How in the hell did she manage to get in the middle of one?

The siren was off, but the lights flashed as Otis sped west on I-40. Kent and Cooper were headed back to Edmond and Oklahoma City, respectively. He was angry and concerned, hoping to see Sydney's green CR-V when he reached the rest stop on the other side of the highway.

He drove past, then made a U-turn farther along, reserved for official vehicles. The CR-V was nowhere in sight. He pulled into a parking spot that would be visible to anyone heading east, turned off the motor, and got out. The wind was strong, gusting hard, and he turned his back to the black SUV and leaned against the door.

He checked his phone to see if Sydney had called. He called his office to let them know where he was and got several messages. He made two calls, then checked the time. He'd been waiting nearly fifteen minutes. Something was wrong. There was no answer when he tried Sydney's number.

Sydney reached the spot where she could steer the car back onto the pavement. At least she was pretty certain this was it. Dust still beat against the car and windshield. As she started to steer left, the chopper appeared, nearly setting down in that exact spot. She couldn't go that way, so she kept heading straight ahead.

A dirt road appeared, heading off to the right. The chopper settled near the ground, blocking her way onto the highway. Heading south wasn't exactly a good move, but if she stayed on the side of the road, she would eventually become stuck.

The car vibrated as she sped along the washboard of a road. It sounded as if more rattles were being made with each bump. Dust rose behind her like a rooster tail, hiding the chopper. Dust floated forward, making her feel as if she drove in a whirlwind that carried her along. The sound of the wheels on the road surrounded her. Would she hear the chopper if it came near again?

When it reappeared, it was out of the dust and alarmingly close.

Either Carly didn't see the car clearly, or she was getting more and more reckless. One of the skids slid across the top of the car. The sound filled the inside of the car, nearly drowning out that of the blades. Sydney expected to look up and see daylight. She whipped the steering left, throwing the car into a bootleg turn, and headed back through the cloud of dust. Her surprise at actually making the maneuver so many years after learning how to do it would have to wait until later. If there was a later.

The chopper came at her from the left this time. She could see Carly and Franklin through the haze. His eyes were wide, and his white-knuckles on the hand grip were plain to see. Her eyes were slits, her jaws clenched so tightly her mouth was a red slit just above her chin.

One of the skids caught the roof again. The last thing Sydney saw as the CR-V leaned dangerously to the right was the surprised expression on Carly's face.

Otis saw smoke to the west, about ten or twelve miles away. His instinct told him he better check it out.

Driving like a bat out of hell, he bounced across the ditch of the median, squealing tires as he came around onto the westbound side of the Interstate. He turned off onto the county road that led toward Corn, lights flashing, siren wailing. He was surprised when he realized that the smoke came from off the two-lane highway.

He turned left onto the dirt road. The column of smoke rose to the south. He saw the fire before he saw the green CR-V lying on its side a short distance away.

CHAPTER 19

The black SUV slid to a stop as Otis slammed on the brakes. He climbed out, at the same time shouting his location into the cell phone. When he received confirmation, he threw the phone on the seat. The only sound was the wind and the roar of the fire engulfing the chopper. The CR-V had flipped and lay on its top. He ran to the driver's side of the car. On his knees, he looked in. Sydney hung upside down, held by the shoulder harness. The air bag hung loosely over the steering wheel. He pulled on the door with all his might, but it wouldn't open.

Giving that up, he got a tire iron out of his SUV and broke the window, trying to be careful not to send glass flying into her face. He pulled the glass outward with the tire iron once he'd made a hole. The whole window was shattered, and most of it came away in a limp sheet. Traces of blood from his hands streaked across it.

With the chopper on fire, he feared a spark might ignite the gas leaking from the CR-V. He might otherwise have waited for a fire department crew to handle her extraction. Waiting wasn't an option this time.

He reached in and, with an arm around Sydney's shoulders, tried to release the shoulder harness. It was also jammed. He pulled a Buck knife from the holster on his belt and sliced the strap. It took two swipes of the sharp blade. When it parted, Sydney's full weight dropped onto his arm. Tossing the knife away, Otis began pulling her free, working as fast as he could, mindful of her neck and back.

When he finally freed her, he dragged her away from the wreck. He could have picked her up easily but didn't want to chance causing further injury.

He knelt beside her and leaned down with his cheek close to her nose and mouth. He thought he detected a slight breath. Her carotid artery pulsed under his fingertips. With a sigh, he sat back on his heels. She was alive. How badly she was injured wasn't readily apparent.

A dark bruise already showed on the bridge of her nose where her sunglasses must have been jammed against her by the air bag. He took off his heavy coat and spread it over her, then went to the SUV and grabbed the water bottle he always carried. Kneeling beside her again, he poured a little water into his hand, then wiped her face, especially her lips, moistening them. Her tongue slipped between her lips, licking the moisture.

After that, she lay still. Otis turned to see the flames thrusting into the air, smoke rising higher and higher. No one inside could have survived. Still, he made himself get to his feet and walk around the machine. The tail number was obscured; by the time the fire was put out, it would be gone. Footprints led away from the side which was hidden from his view as he worked to save Sydney's life.

For a moment, he stood looking off in the direction in which the footprints led. Nothing moved. Was it possible that someone got out? If so, where were they now? A copse of trees stood in the distance. A ditch or stream bed ran along at a slight angle, left to right. Just then, he heard sirens coming his way. He walked back to Sydney.

Smoke and flames still rose from the blackened hulk. All of the fire extinguishers from the cars were not enough to put the fire out. Otis thought he saw at least one body, but the heat was still too intense to get close. Everything was burned beyond recognition.

The ambulance sped away toward Oklahoma City. Sydney suffered a concussion but was conscious. Her right ankle hurt, whether it was broken or sprained they wouldn't know until it was x-rayed.

As first on the scene, he asked one of the troopers who responded to his call to follow the footprints leading away from the chopper. Even though Otis was out of his jurisdiction, the trooper complied. Otis actually wanted to go himself, but he also needed to wait for the forensics team.

A pumper truck arrived from one of the nearby fire departments, and another truck came in soon after. They doused the fire, steam and smoke rising into the blue sky, drifting east in the prevailing wind. Everything was still too hot to touch, but he got as close as he could and looked over the remains.

As he expected, the tail number was gone. The FAA would have to work that out. It was the only thing that might identify either the owner of the chopper or who flew it.

It was dark by the time he got to the hospital to check on Sydney. The nurses told him that she was going to be all right; the ankle injury was a sprain, but the air bag broke a bone in her hand and her ribs were bruised. After treatment, she had insisted on taking a shower before getting into the bed, where she fell asleep quickly. Pain pills helped.

He tiptoed into her room.

"It's all right, Otis. I'm awake." She groaned as she tried to straighten up in bed. "You're too big to be tiptoeing."

He grinned. "True." He pulled a chair closer to the bed and sat down. "Do you remember what happened?"

"I think so. I remember the chopper chasing me, then appearing suddenly and very close in the dust the car was throwing into the air. Not a great deal after that, though. I think one of the skids caught the car."

"Probably."

"The chopper? Did they get away?"

"No. The chopper crashed and burned."

"Really?"

"Not much left except a blackened hulk."

"Franklin and Amador were both killed?"

"They were both in the chopper?"

"Yes, they got close enough I could see them. The man they called Saw was there, too."

"We can't confirm their deaths."

"Why?"

"The fire was so intense. There just isn't much left. We think we found the remains of at least one person, but until the M.E. takes a look, we don't know who it was or if others were in the chopper when it went down."

She shuddered and closed her eyes.

"You need your sleep," Otis said. "I'm glad you're all right."

"Thanks. I think I might need another pain pill before I can go to sleep."

"I'll tell the nurse. Good night, Sydney."

"'Night, Otis."

She woke in the dead of night. Her scream woke her. The skid of the helicopter came through the open window of the car and hooked the steering wheel. She couldn't get it loose or steer the car. She screamed. Was it only in her nightmare?

Lying there, listening to the silence, she waited to see if anyone came. If she had screamed aloud, surely someone would. No one appeared.

Her eyes closed, and once again she slept.

Otis drove her home three days later. The doctors wanted her to rest for a week, which wasn't hard to do since she had no transportation. Julia came by with a big container of her potato soup. They joked about Sydney's clumsiness; her body was so stiff and sore, making every movement painful.

They had operated on her right hand and it was wrapped in a brace of sorts. Her ankle was wrapped in stretch bandages. She was woozy from the pain pills, although she stopped taking them that morning. She hated their effect on her consciousness. However, if the pain became too much, she promised to take the pills, hoping it wouldn't be necessary.

"I suppose you called Ben," Julia said.

"Yes, as soon as I was able to speak coherently. Otis already called him to reassure him that I was all right. Just a little banged up."

"What did Ben say?"

"He's making arrangements to get here the first of next week. We weren't planning on his coming out yet, but he insisted. I couldn't tell if he was angry, upset, or ... I don't know.

He calmed down and said how worried he was. And that I was to take it easy until he gets here."

"What about after he gets here?" Julia said with an impish grin.

"I guess we have to wait and see."

Sydney grinned, grateful that her friend could make a joke about anything right now. This mystery wasn't supposed to be a danger to her, or anyone else for that matter. Except, of course, to the two people who were murdered. Danger was always hovering above the fray, so to speak, and she'd chosen to ignore it. After ending up in the hospital, she promised herself, no more. She was done with murder and mysteries except for what she found in the archives. Let them stay there from now on.

CHAPTER 20

Sydney dished up the last of the potato soup. It was only Friday, but she was already feeling restless. The next order of business should be buying a new car, but the car rental company wasn't delivering a vehicle until tomorrow.

Daytime television was abysmal, and her mood wasn't helped when Dr. Arnold called and reamed her out for bringing more notoriety to the archives.

"Eleanor is most upset," he said. When she was upset, Dr. Arnold was upset.

She wanted to tell him to go to hell, especially since he didn't ask how she was. She managed to listen quietly, agreeing with everything he said and promising not to get involved in anything more.

She meant to never get into such trouble again.

The phone rang. It was Otis calling to see if he could come over. "Did you write up what you remember about that day?" he asked.

"Yes. It's ready for you. There are a few gaps, but I might be able to remember more later on."

"Okay. I'll be there within the hour."

"I could just email it." She wasn't sure that she wanted company.

"Yeah, but I want to read it and then discuss it. You might remember other details."

She agreed, even though there couldn't be much more to remember. It was time to get dressed. Every muscle and joint complained as she pulled on sweat pants and a sweat shirt. The pain was less than the day before. Healing was going to be slow in spite of the mild exercises the doctor recommended she do. The splint on her hand wouldn't come off for another week. It made showering awkward, but she worked with getting a plastic bag over the hand, sealed with some tape. Getting it all arranged felt like a great accomplishment.

The bandage on her left ankle could be taken off when she bathed but replaced immediately once she was dried off. Again, she was very careful, as the ankle sprain made standing uncomfortable, and the only shoes she could wear were slippers. She hated being incapacitated, especially now that she felt better overall and badly needed to get groceries.

The phone rang again. This time it was Julia calling to see if she needed anything.

"I need groceries. Can you take me to the store?"

"I'll pick up whatever you need. You need to rest."

"I'm tired of resting." Sydney heard the petulance in her own voice and cleared her throat.

"I know, but I'm really busy here, and it will be late when I get away. It would be easier for me to just get a list and stop on my way there."

That meant only those things available in the local convenience store. They carried a few more grocery items than most, sort of like the corner groceries Sydney knew as a child.

"I'll make a list and call you back. Or email it to you."

"Yeah, email it."

"Thanks, Julia."

"You're welcome."

The call disconnected and Sydney put the handset in the cradle. She was reclining on the sofa, the TV on, but the sound off. She reached for the remote control just as someone knocked on the door. Otis sure took his time getting there. She moved Lewis out of the way, reached for the crutches lying across the ottoman, and hoisted herself up, careful not to put any weight on the injured ankle. Slowly, she made her way toward the door. Using crutches was an acquired skill, one not yet mastered.

She was halfway between the door and the sofa when the door crashed inward. Later, she realized that her first thought was, "Oh, no. Not again." The door which had taken a beating in the past shattered, pieces hanging in place.

She turned, teetered, managed two steps toward the bedroom. Suddenly grabbed from behind, she was picked up. One crutch dropped away while she clung to the other. Any weapon at hand.

She was thrown onto the sofa. Only then did she see that the man was Saw, the bigger of the two men encountered before. He was in the chopper when it went down. She saw him climb in with Franklin.

Still standing in the doorway, Carly Amador looked around the room, ignoring Sydney for the moment. How did she and Saw get out of the chopper when it crashed?

Neither of them escaped without injury. Clear burn marks and cuts and scratches marred both of their faces and hands. Carly's gaze came to rest on Sydney in her examination of the living room.

"You, someone who lives like this, has come close to bringing me down," Carly said. "I am so much more than you are, yet you thought you would beat me."

Sydney looked up at Saw standing over her, then back at Carly. "I don't know what you mean. I don't know anything about you or Franklin or Denton Oil."

"Sure, you do. You looked through our financials. You broke into our computers and found … let's just say, compromising documents."

"But I didn't. All I ever did was research the O'Kelleys."

Was Carly talking about the research that Ben did? He wouldn't have broken into the company computers. He probably wouldn't even know how.

"Of course, you did. Who else would do that?"

"You must have enemies."

Carly chuckled. "A few."

"Franklin must have brought a few with him, from what I read about him."

"So, you admit checking us out."

"Only as the company pertained to Francine."

"Yes, she was a problem. As for Franklin! He had enemies. Most of them deserved. But he was very useful in getting Denton more financially stable."

"Was it his idea to get the land in Delhi?"

"We would have been satisfied with the oil rights, but he got greedy. He was going to put the land in his name, then sell the drilling rights to the company."

"I'm sorry he's dead," Sydney said, wondering if Carly was also sorry.

"He served his purpose. In the end, he became a liability."

"He was your lover."

"How do you ..." She waved a hand as if the question was unimportant. "A very good lover, at that." She looked over at Saw. "It's time to go."

He reached out to pick up Sydney.

"I need my coat if we're going outside."

"No. We won't be going very far."

Sydney raised the crutch to hit Saw, but he grabbed it with one of his large hands and pushed the end to the floor, where he put his foot on it, forcing her to let go. As he picked her up, she groped at the table beside the sofa. Her hand grasped a pencil. Clutching it in her fist, she held it close to her chest. His hold on her made her ribs hurt, and she gritted her teeth.

Carly led the way through the gaping doorway to a waiting black limousine. Saw set her onto the back seat, then climbed in and sat across from her. Carly sat beside her.

"Let's go, Aldo," she said. The limo pulled away from the curb. The driver looked very much like Saw's earlier companion.

As they drove through the neighborhood and turned toward downtown, she prayed that they would pass Otis or Julia on their way to her house. That couldn't help, though. The windows were too dark to see in. Pretending to adjust her seat, she stuck the pencil in the front pocket of her pants. What good it might do was a mystery.

They headed through town, toward I-35. Sydney thought she saw Otis's black SUV turning a corner, heading in the direction of her house, but she couldn't be certain it was he.

"What happens now?" Sydney asked.

Carly looked out the window, as if ignoring the question. Finally, she turned toward Sydney. "You will simply disappear. With you out of the way, I will simply go back to my life."

"The sheriff has all the details of what happened. I saw you and Franklin in the chopper. Saw, too."

"You made a statement, of course, but it won't have the effect of corroborating testimony. I have good lawyers."

"But records will show that you hired the chopper."

"And I will swear that Franklin was in it. No one else was found, so proving I was there will be difficult at best."

"How did you and Saw get out of the chopper?"

"When it started out of control, we jumped out. It wasn't easy, and we were lucky. I guess the smoke and everything helped hide us. The explosion caught us, thus the burns you see."

She seemed to have no idea that Sydney was unconscious when the car wrecked.

"Won't your injuries help to prove you were in the chopper, then?" Sydney said.

"They can be explained by a number of things. It's all circumstantial at best. With you gone, there's very little they can do."

Sydney shifted positions again and winced at the tenderness of her ribs. The overall soreness of her body might make it difficult to fight back. Her ankle was too bad to walk on. If the opportunity came, would she be able to fight back or run away?

The limo ran smoothly up the highway, heading north. After about ten minutes, it pulled off onto an exit ramp. The exit sign was hard to see from the back seat. The winter landscape flashed by in a blur. The road seemed smooth, although that might be due to the quality of the limo's suspension.

Did Carly pick this area earlier, or was it random? Sydney could only guess where they were or what was to happen to her. As surreptitiously as possible, she tried the door handle, but it was locked and there was no button or switch to unlock it.

Otis was probably at her house by now, wondering what the hell happened. The broken door would tell him she was in trouble, but not where she was. How could he possibly find her in time?

Otis got out of the SUV slowly, pulling his Glock free at the same time. Even from the curb it was clear that the door was left open. As he walked up the steps, he feared that Sydney was gone. Whether taken by someone associated with Carly Amador or by her, Sydney hadn't left voluntarily. Once inside, his worst fears were confirmed. Sydney was gone and the whole front door was a mess. Both crutches lay on the floor of the living room along with parts of the door and door frame.

He called his office and told Sharon to get in touch with Kent and have him come out and canvas the neighborhood. Although it was a long shot, he called the post office, asking for George, the carrier who delivered to that area.

"Have him call me right away," he told the supervisor. "It's a matter of life and death."

Although he worked in just one part of town, George knew everyone in Gansel. If he saw a strange vehicle in the area, he would remember it.

Kent arrived and started with the houses where cars were parked, either on the street or in driveways. Before he finished, George called back.

"Hey, Otis. What's up?"

"Hey, George. Did you by chance see a strange vehicle in the northwest neighborhoods?"

"Well ..."

The line went silent for the space of several heartbeats. Otis knew that George was searching his memory, sorting out the things he'd seen. So, he waited without prodding.

"There was a fancy limousine less than an hour ago. I was on my way into that area, and it came zooming out. Like they were in a real hurry."

"Could you see anyone inside?"

"No, them windows were much too dark. Couldn't see anything."

"Not even the number of people inside?"

"Nuh-uh."

"Did it have an Oklahoma license?"

"Yep." He gave Otis the number. His memory for figures was well known.

"Thanks, George."

"Any time."

Otis disconnected, then dialed the State Police office. When the dispatcher answered, he asked for Sergeant Greer.

"What's up, Otis?"

"I need a favor."

"Again?" Greer chuckled.

"Yeah, it's another emergency. I have a possible kidnapping, probably looking for a black limousine, Oklahoma license." He quoted the number from memory.

"Do you want to be picked up?"

"Yes. I'm not sure what we're looking for, so we will have to make a wide sweep of interstate and county roads." He gave Sydney's address, letting Greer know that there was an empty field behind the house.

"Gimme a minute."

The line went silent. Otis paced from the living room to the kitchen and back. Greer came back on the line.

"Done."

"Thanks. I owe you."

"I'll collect. We've notified rolling units to be on the lookout, so watch for them."

"Will do."

Otis thanked Greer and disconnected. He went outside to see Kent just walking back.

"Nothing," the deputy said. "Most people aren't home."

Any kind of limousine was a rare sight in Gansel. People would have noticed. But there was no way to ask everyone in town. He told Kent to head east out of town toward the interstate and look for anyone working outside. "If you find anyone, ask them if they saw the limousine. If there's no one, head west and do the same. I suspect they would take the interstate first to get some distance away fast. But that might be wrong."

Just then, the sound of an approaching helicopter came from the north. Both men looked up to see it heading for the field behind the house.

"Good luck," Kent said and headed for his SUV. Otis went around the house and through the gate in the back fence. The chopper landed, and they were soon on their way east.

The limo sped on, heading farther and farther into the countryside. No one spoke. What was there to say? Sydney could beg for her life. Carly could gloat. So far, Saw remained silent.

Suddenly, Carly leaned forward. "Here," she said to Saw, who turned and said something to Aldo. A dirt road crossed the paved road they were on, and he turned right. They drove on, not far this time, and the car pulled into a copse of oak trees. Saw climbed out, and Carly motioned for Sydney to follow. She tried, but the sore ankle wouldn't support her.

Saw came around to her side of the car and reached in to pick her up. Both times he carried her, it was as if she was light as a feather. After feeling so heavy for a number of years, it was a very odd experience.

Carly got out of the car and walked through the trees and into the open field. The wind was cold, and somewhere a hawk screeched. Sydney shivered as Saw held her, waiting for Carly to give him instructions. His body was warm against her side. His arms were warm as they cradled her.

"Oh, look," Carly called out. "It's a cemetery. This will do."

Saw followed the path his boss took.

"Here," she said.

He set Sydney on a low stone marker. They were in a family burial ground with seven markers, some tipped over or leaning, three standing straight up. All but one was worn, the lettering nearly gone. People were buried here a long time ago. The stone she sat on was upright, and cold under her butt. Without the warmth of Saw's body, the cold penetrated even more. She folded her arms over her chest, wishing they had let her get her coat to make this all less painful. Until the end.

It appeared that her discomfort wouldn't last much longer.

"This place has been abandoned for a long time," Carly said, looking around them. "The trees are between here and the road. And there's no one to hear, not for miles and miles."

The sound of a vehicle on the road coming from the opposite direction of the paved road put the lie to her words. As the pickup truck came abreast of the trees, it crunched to a stop.

They couldn't see it for the trees, but they heard the door slam shut.

A man who looked about fifty and was probably a farmer or rancher walked toward them his expression friendly. He waved and Carly waved back. He must not have seen Aldo in the limo.

"Don't do or say anything," she said to Sydney. "If you do, he's dead."

"Hi, there," the newcomer said.

"Hi," Carly said.

"Can I help you folks?"

"No, sir. We're just looking around. Came across this old cemetery and thought we'd take a look."

The man nodded, as he looked at Sydney with a frown. "You'll catch your death," he said.

"We won't be long," Carly said. "She's very warm-natured."

Sydney nodded agreement, but she was visibly shivering. She could think of nothing to say that would alert him but not her captors. Anything might give the two a reason to shoot him, and she must avoid that at all cost.

"Is this your land?" Carly said, trying to distract the man from Sydney.

"No, it doesn't belong to anyone anymore. Abandoned for a long time. My farm is further back." He motioned vaguely down the road. "I've got a coat in the truck if you need it."

Saw reached inside his jacket. Carly was about to nod to him.

Sydney shook her head. "I'm fine. I appreciate your concern."

"Okay, if you say so." He turned to Carly. "You folks take care now." He turned and walked way. Sydney felt a strange blend of relief and despair.

"The limo is owned by Denton Oil. They have a transponder on board."

Otis nodded. That would make it possible to find the damned thing. "How did you get the company to cooperate?"

"Told them their CEO was missing, possibly kidnapped. The dispatcher will relay their position."

The pilot turned the chopper northeast. Otis scanned the

ground in general, looking for dust on the back roads, and specifically for a black limo. It was dust he saw first. The limo became clear when he raised the binoculars and adjusted them.

"There it is," he said, pointing.

"Got it," the pilot said after a moment. "The rolling units are on their way."

Otis nodded, keeping his eyes on the vehicle all the while. It sat just off the dirt road near a bunch of trees. It looked like it was the blue pickup sitting right behind it that raised the dust. With the binoculars, he could make out four people.

"Don't spook 'em until we have cars in the area," Otis said.

"Right."

They hovered above and to the south of the car. Otis watched them while the pilot looked for state police cars.

"They're closing in," the pilot said. They'll let us know when they have 'em."

CHAPTER 21

"Oh, just one thing," Carly called after the man.

Saw took his hand from inside his jacket, the pistol pointing at the man. He automatically raised his hands, never taking his eyes from Saw.

"I'm afraid you've seen too much."

He didn't say anything, didn't even seem frightened. Probably a veteran of one of America's wars, where he faced down more than one gun.

Carly reached for Saw's gun. "Go tell Aldo to hide the pickup somewhere. Not too far away, so he can walk back.

The big man disappeared, leaving his boss standing there with murder in her eyes. The door of the pickup slammed, the motor started up, and it drove away in the same direction it was going before. There were other groups of trees along the way, enough in which to hide the pickup.

"You can't kill him," Sydney said. "He won't tell anyone he saw you even if my body is found. He hasn't done anything."

Her lips were so cold that the words were slightly slurred. They understood her meaning, though. Carly looked around as Saw returned.

Saw looked to Carly, and she nodded.

Sydney gave up in her heart. There was no way to escape, no way to save herself or the man. He stood perfectly still, his hands in the air, seeming to study the situation. She'd never seen anyone so calm in a life and death situation. As she concentrated on him, ignoring the two who intended to kill her, she realized why. He wore a jacket with patches that showed he was a prisoner of war. Which war she couldn't tell but, the man had stared death down before.

"We'll wait until Aldo gets back," Carly was saying. "Meanwhile, you'd better have a seat," she added, addressing the stranger.

A nearly upright tombstone stood on the other side of Sydney. As he walked past her, he asked in a low voice, "Can you run?"

"No," she whispered, looking up at him so that he could see the word on her lips. "Sorry," she said a bit louder.

"No talking," Carly said, waving the gun in her direction. She handed it back to Saw.

After several minutes of silence, they all heard the door of the limo shut.

Aldo must be back, Sydney thought.

"Now we can get down to business," Carly said. "None of this was ever supposed to get so complicated," she continued, looking at Sydney. "I don't have anything against either of you personally. I hope you …"

The limo suddenly appeared coming around the trees, heading straight for them. It bounced over the uneven ground, gaining speed.

"What the …" Saw shouted. "Aldo! What the fuck?"

The car was too near to argue, and the two ran out of the way. It stopped between them and the two prisoners. The back door opened.

"Get in," a voice yelled.

Not waiting to be told twice, the man went to Sydney and helped her into the car. They climbed in, Sydney first, and the car backed up before they were seated properly. A huge amount of dust rose in the air, too much to have been raised by the car.

Helicopter, Sydney realized.

The limo was soundproofed, but they still heard the whoosh, whoosh of the rotor blades. She thought she heard a voice over a loudspeaker of some sort. The limo slammed to a stop, and she was thrown against the seat across the back. She and the man ended up in a tangle of arms and legs. When they were able to untangle, each of them apologized.

The window between the driver and the back whined down.

"You two all right back there?"

"Yes, thanks," Sydney said.

"Who ..."

He opened the door and was gone before she could see who asked.

Sydney slid to the door and opened it.

"You might better wait," the man said. "No tellin' what's happenin'."

"Thanks, but ..."

She put her good foot on the ground and used the door to pull herself out and up. The limo sat across the dirt road. Behind it, Carly and Saw raised their hands. Two state troopers held them at gunpoint. A helicopter sat in the field beyond them. Otis climbed out and walked toward them.

CHAPTER 22

Sydney sat quietly in the back seat of the limousine, warmed now by the man's jacket. His name was David Freeman. He had served in Afghanistan in the first Middle East war. They exchanged contact information, but that was all she learned.

Although his life was as much in danger as hers, she felt that he saved her. His showing up when he did gave Otis and the State Police time to catch up to them, for which she would always be grateful.

Carly and Saw sat in the back of separate squad cars. Aldo was being brought back. He was handcuffed and looked sullen. Otis oversaw everything, having first made certain that Sydney was okay.

As she waited for transportation home, she tried to work out why Carly thought she was a danger to her plans. There was something about tapping into the corporate computers, which Sydney couldn't do if she wanted to. Ben wouldn't do that on principle, even if he knew how.

"Looks like we're 'bout ready," a familiar voice said.

She looked up at Otis and smiled. "I'm not quite sure where I'm going," she said. "The house isn't in any shape for me to stay there right now. And I can't drive. Well, I don't have anything to drive, do I?" She rambled on for a while, Otis listening patiently.

"At least, I won't have to take you to the hospital this time," he said.

She laughed. "True."

She put her hands in the pockets of her sweat pants, surprised to find the pencil still there. Pulling it out, she showed it to Otis.

"What's that for?"

"I have no idea," she said.

She stood on her good foot. Otis picked her up and walked toward another squad car.

"I called Julia and told her you need a place to stay. She said to bring you there for the time being."

Sydney appreciated Julia's generosity, but she hated to impose. There were no motels or hotels in Gansel, so there was little choice. She'd make it up to her somehow.

CHAPTER 23

Ben tested the new door and decided it was a good, solid job. He had arrived two days after Sydney's latest adventure. She was prepared for his anger and concern, but he stayed very low-key and very helpful, insisting that she stay off her feet as much as possible.

Coffee was ready, and they sat and discussed what had happened. She guessed that Patrick found out about the gold and Denton Oil's interest in the oil rights to the old farm. If he could find the gold, he could claim the land outright, sell the rights, and be set for life.

Francine–or Doris–must have found out that much. She may have made a deal with Franklin to help him get title to the land or find the gold. Having seen her with Saw, Sydney knew that she was involved from the beginning. Carly was the wild card.

The gold was still missing, if it existed, but if everyone was patient, the storage locker would be identified, at least, and the gold might actually be there. It was a lot of money with no one to claim it now. It would have been nice for there to have been a reward Sydney could claim.

"That would help with the new house," Ben said.

She agreed, a bit surprised at his words. If he accepted that she was planning on staying in Gansel for a while, maybe he was becoming more accepting of his moving there, at least part of the year.

Suddenly the walls of the house rattled. Then a dull boom. Lewis, on his way to the bedroom, stopped with one paw raised. Sydney froze. When the shaking stopped, she realized that it was only a second or two, although it felt longer.

"What was that?"

Ben smiled. "An earthquake."

"Really? Here in Oklahoma? I guess living in California, you'd know."

"Is that the first you've felt?"

"I think I felt one before, when I lived back east, but never here."

"It's probably just a one-time thing."

"I should hope so. There aren't any fault lines through here, I don't think."

He shrugged.

"Maybe I should check the archives."

"Later. Right now, lunch is ready."

He came over to help her with the crutches. As she stood, she grabbed hold of his hand and squeezed.

"Thank you," she said.

He hugged her while supporting her. "I should have come sooner."

"You're here, now."

He laughed. "Sounds like a movie script."

"Yeah, but sometimes truth is stranger than fiction."

"I'm beginning to learn that big time."

They made their way into the kitchen where Ben set up lunch for them. She was getting the hang of the crutches, but enjoyed his warm arms helping her get around..

ABOUT THE AUTHOR

Cary Osborne's tastes have always been eclectic, due to her varied background. Because of that, she has written in several genres, including science fiction, fantasy, and horror. Recently, she delved into the fictional world of mysteries. She won an honorable mention and was a finalist in the Writers of the Future Contest for short stories. Having lived all over the country, she recently moved from New Mexico to Oklahoma.

Book List:

The Iroshi Trilogy
Iroshi
The Glaive
Persea

The Deathweave Series
Deathweave
Darkloom

The Sydney St. John Mysteries
Oklahoma Winds
Black Ice
Saving Souls

Winter Queen

Curious about other Crossroad Press books?
Stop by our site:
http://store.crossroadpress.com
We offer quality writing
in digital, audio, and print formats.

Enter the code FIRSTBOOK
to get 20% off your first order from our store!
Stop by today!